Jailed for Life

A Reporter's Prison Notes

TITLES IN THE HEINEMANN FRONTLINE SERIES

Upper Level

Cyprian Ekwensi: *For A Roll of Parchment*
Patrick Fagbola: *Kaduna Mafia*
Niyi Osundare: *The Eye of the Earth* (Joint-Winner of the 1986
Commonwealth Poetry Prize)
Rose Njoku: *Withstand the Storm*
Jeremiah Essien: *In the Shadow of Death*
Okinba Launko: *Minted Coins*: (Winner of the Africa Zone of 1988
Dillions Commonwealth Poetry Prize)
Chinua Achebe: *Anthills of the Savannah*
Tess Onwueme: The *Reign of Wazobia and other Plays*
Atabo Oko: *The Secret of the Sheik*
Tess Onwueme: *Legacies* (a play)
Niyi Osundare: *Songs of the Season* (poems)
Niyi Osundare: *Midlife* (poems)
Niyi Osundare: *Horses of Memory* (poems)
Afolabi A Adio-Moses: *Flashes of Ideas and Reflections (poems)*
Tolu Ajayi: *The Ghost of a Millionaire*
Oladele Akadiri: *A Sin in the Convent*
Bridget Nwankwo: *Drums of Destiny*
Iyorwuese H. Hagher: *Mulkin Mata* (a play)
Sola Osofisan: *Darksongs* (Winner, 1990 ANA Poetry Prize)
Sola Osofisan: *The Living and The Dead* (Winner, 1990 ANA Prose
Prize)
Femi Osofisan: *Once Upon Four Robbers* (a play)
Femi Osofisan: *Yungba Yungba and the Dance Contest*
Stella Oyedepo: *Beyond the Dark Tunnel* (a play)
Chukwuemeka Ike: *The Search*
Chukwuemeka Ike: *The Naked Gods*
Chukwuemeka Ike: *The Chicken Chasers*
Stella Oyedepo: *The Greatest Gift* (a play)
ANA / British Council: *Five Plays* (Winner, 1989 ANA Drama Prize)
Patrick Idahosa: *Truth and Tragedy*
Chidi Ikonne: *Our Land*
Rasheed Gbadamosi: *Sunset Over Nairobi*
Femi Osofisan: *Aringindin and the Nightwatchmen*
Omowunmi Segun: *The Third Dimple* (Winner, 1991 ANA Prose Prize)

Phanuel Akubueze Egejuru: *The Seed Yams Have Been Eaten*
Ralph Opara: *It Never Happened to Me*
I.N.C. Aniebo: *Rearguard Actions* (Winner, 1998 ANA Prose Prize)
John Munonye: *A Kind of Fool*
Akinwumi Isola: *Madam Tinubu* (play)
Lupenga Mphande: *Crackle at Midnight* (poems)
Tanure Ojaide: *Invoking the Warrior Spirit* (poems)
Charles Bodunde: *Nectar Pots* (poems)
Kunle Ajibade: *Jailed for Life – A Reporter's Prison Notes*

Intermediate Level
Chinelo Achebe: *The Last Laugh and Other Stories*
Tess Onwueme: *Ban Empty Barn and Other Plays*
Tess Onwueme: *Mirror for Campus* (a play)
Tess Onwueme: *The Trial of the Beautiful Ones* (a play)
S. Arogbofa: *Agidi Sours* (a play)
S. Arogbofa: *A Celebration of Love*
S. Arogbofa: *A Game of Power*
Ola Rotimi: *A Tragedy of the Ruled* (a play)
F. Aig-Imoukhuede: *Pidgin Stew and Sufferhead* (poems)
Kathleen Egbuna: *That Wartime*
M. J. Akpabio: *A Trip to the Atlantic*
T. M. Aluko: *First Year at State College*
Tony Marinho: *The Epidemic*
Clement Okosun: *A Child with a Child*
Cyprian Ekwensi: *Motherless Baby*
Felicia Onyewadume: *First Term at School*
Felicia Onyewadume: *Echoes of Hard Times and other plays*
Mercy Nwanne Anya: *Tell Me More*

Junior Level
A.O. Oyekanmi: *The Lion and the Hare*
Augustus Adebayo: *Once Upon a Village*
Chinua Achebe: *Chike and the River*
Chinwe M. Agbakoba: *Mma and Nkita*
Chinwe M. Agbakoba: *Ejiofor and His Mother*
Margaret Brook: *The Play for Yejide*
Cyprian Ekwensi: *Gone to Mecca*
Cyprian Ekwensi: *Passport of Mallam Ilia*

Jailed for Life

A Reporter's Prison Notes

Kunle Ajibade

Heinemann Educational Books (Nigeria) Plc

HEINEMANN EDUCATIONAL BOOKS (NIGERIA) PLC
Head Office: 1 Ighodaro Road, Jericho, P.M.B. 5205, Ibadan
Phone: (02) 2412268, 2410943, 2411213; *Fax:* (02) 2411089, 2413237
E-mail: info@heinemannbooks.com
               heinemannbooks@yahoo.com
Website: http://www.heinemannbooks.com

Area Offices and Branches
Abeokuta . Akure . Bauchi . Benin City . Calabar . Enugu . Ibadan
Ikeja . Ilorin . Jos . Kano . Katsina . Maiduguri . Makurdi . Minna
Owerri . Port Harcourt . Sokoto . Uyo . Yola . Zaria

ISBN 978 129 559 7

© Kunle Ajibade 2003
First published 2003

Printed by Planet Press Limited, Lagos.

To Bunmi for bearing the ordeals of my enforced
absence with exemplary resilience.

Unending
Thanks

Between May 23, 1995 and July 20, 1998, I languished behind bars for an offence I did not commit. As soon as I regained my freedom, Pen Center USA West in Los Angeles showed a special interest in the notes that I began sketching clandestinely in Makurdi Prison on August 14, 1996. It, therefore, recommended me for the 1998/1999 Feuchtwanger Fellowship of Villa Aurora, the Foundation for European-American Relations*.

I spent ten months of a very rewarding intellectual engagement in Los Angeles. The prestigious Paul Getty Research Institute housed me in its apartments to read, reflect, relax with endless movies, write and give talks. I remember L.A. with fondness now because it is also the city in which I was properly reunited with my family after the agonising years of separation.

I thank Eric Lax, Sherrill Britton, Larry Siems, Deborah Jones, Judy Molland, Sandra Mills, Aimee Liu, Wendy Belcher, Lili Barsha, Kathryn Phillips and other active members of the Pen Center USA West for recommending me for the fellowship. I am grateful to Dagmar Spira, then Director of Villa Aurora and Petra Larsen, her assistant, who made the fellowship possible; and Dr. Joachim Bernauer, the new Director, and Babett Sparr, his assistant, who administered it after Dagmar had left the Villa. I thank Michael Roth of Paul Getty Research Institute and Karen Sexton-Josephs, the cheerful woman in charge of the Getty Scholars' apartments, for their kindness. I also thank Nuno Philips, Dr. Christopher Ajigbotafe and Dr. Ade Adelekan, who made sure

---

* The Villa is an endowment of Lion Feuchtwanger, a notable German writer, to keep alive the memory of the artists who fled Germany during the Nazi regime.

that I had comprehensive medical check up at their own expense as soon as I got to Los Angeles.

I will remain ever grateful to Professors Wole Soyinka, Biodun Jeyifo, Olatunji Dare, Tejumola Olaniyan and Femi Taiwo who helped to nourish my lean draft with their deep insights. I also owe Moji Olaniyan, Siobhan Dowd, Judy Molland, Bunmi Ajibade, Larry Siems, Akin Adesokan, Odia Ofeimun, Adewale Maja-Pearce, Femi Falana, Becky Clarke, Adeolu Ademoyo, Buky Onabanjo, Ifeanyi Uddin, Morenike Ransome-Kuti, Irene Staunton and Toun Onabanjo a debt of gratitude for their constructive criticisms of some of my inelegant renderings. Inevitably, I remain responsible for all stubborn stylistic infelicities that the book may still contain, as well as for my opinion of some personalities and institutions.

Chief Aigboje Higo and Ayo Ojeniyi of Heinemann Nigeria deserve my generous praise for their belief that, as witness of a tyrannical trajectory, my memories should be carefully preserved in the hope that some lessons would be learnt from those long hours of a political tragedy. Olawepo Sogo and Osime Samuel merit my deep appreciation for their meticulous editing of the final draft of the manuscript. I also thank all those anonymous workers in (and for) Heinemann who transformed the typescript to this form.

When I was busy doing other things, I engaged Goodluck Ebelo, Idowu Akinrosoye, Nick Nwafor, Fidelis Soriwei of *TEMPO* and Temitope Ogundokun of *TheNEWS* to help me with the laborious task of transcribing some of the interviews used in this book. I thank them and Gafar Oyewole, who typeset the interviews, for doing the job diligently. Lots of thanks to Solomon Oyeniyi, my personal assistant and driver, for working so hard.

Lastly, I thank all my colleagues who fought gallantly to keep our company going while I was in jail. They risked their lives and those of their families in doing so. This book is indeed a tribute to them in the great expectation that the homeland for which we suffered so much privation would prove worthy of the sacrifice.

K.A.
Lagos, Nigeria
December 20, 2002

From
Wole Soyinka*

Of the many constant faces that simply came to check on my 'state of health', the most wryly bewildered was perhaps Kunle Ajibade, one of the younger generation of adventurous journalists who would himself later undergo the experience of a mock trial and incarceration, without ever losing his sense of the absurd. He came almost ritualistically to my office, sat opposite my desk, and with a mixture of amazement and expectancy on his face, demanded to know:

"But, Prof., why haven't they come for you?"

"Why? Do you want them to?"

"No, but it doesn't make sense. By now they should have taken you in."

"Well, they haven't. So, what's your problem?"

"Well, I don't know why you're still here" he persisted. "It's either you should be heading out of here, or they should be pulling you in."

It was such a persistent puzzle for him that I teased him, insisting that he was hoping for a scoop, making sure that he was on the spot when Abacha's men did come for me. The opposite was true of course, especially as Kunle sometimes took it on himself to censor the odd article or an interview that I granted him, having resolved to protect me against myself! *But Prof.* — he would protest in his high-pitched voice — *if we had published that article as you wrote it, we would have lost you to Abacha right away! And then where would I obtain my interviews?*

---

* This excerpt is taken from the manuscript of Wole Soyinka's forthcoming memoirs with his kind permission.

Kunle of *TheNEWS* magazine was in Abeokuta. He was one of the pioneers of the *samizdat** publication towards which I had nudged his colleagues some years before under Ibrahim Babangida, when the journalists had begun to feel the cutting edge of the smiling teeth of the affable dictator. Babangida's sadistic agents would simply wait until the daily or weekly print run had been completed, then swoop down on editorial houses and cart off their irreplaceable haul. At a lecture at the University of Lagos, I challenged them — *why are you all so unimaginative as to let Babangida's police raid your offices, your printing presses, and cart off copies of your journals without a fight? Have you never heard of underground publishing? Set up more than one editorial office and divide up your pages among various presses. Use fronts. Scatter your editors and let your journalists link up with them by telephone, fax, carrier pigeon, if it comes to that!*

After the lecture, some of them came up to me, eager to learn more. When, two or three years later, Abacha came into power, their *guerrilla tactics* appeared to have been already well honed. The garage behind my office on Lalubu Street was perhaps the earliest mobile office of the *samizdat.* It was already used for clandestine meetings by a youthful group working out their own plans for making Abeokuta a no-go area for Abacha's forces of occupation. There they prepared torrid pamphlets and organised their distribution. The journalists among them put their training to good use. I left the gates to my office compound open when I went home. They came at night and left by morning, leaving the garage clean of any evidence of their nocturnal presence or activities. I never asked him, but remained convinced that Kunle sometimes came into my office so early in the morning because he was coming straight from an all night session with his *samizdat* colleagues.

---

* Government - suppressed but clandestinely printed.

Contents

ONE

~~~~~~~~

Before the
Last Crackdown

Idowu Obasa, one of the founders of Independent Communications Network Limited, publishers of *TheNEWS* magazine, called Lagos from his hotel room on May 22, 1993 to know if the latest edition of the magazine had started circulating. The voice of the security guard who picked the telephone was mournful, 'Armed policemen are here, sir. They've shut down the office, sir!'

Obasa, who had gone to Abeokuta to attend a conference of Chartered Institute of Bankers, left the town abruptly. He thought that maybe by the time he got to Lagos his colleagues would have sorted out the problem.

Now in Lagos: he confirmed that the office of *TheNEWS* was fully occupied by some policemen. When Obasa finally located his colleagues, his anger had not blown over. He did not know that the office would remain besieged for six months.

It transpired that the immediate problem was a cover story in *TheNEWS* on the strategy and tactics of General Ibrahim Babangida's dictatorship, which was written by Ike Okonta, one of our senior writers. That edition also contained 'The Loneliness of a Long Distance Runner', a critical piece on Babangida

by the magazine columnist, Adebayo Williams, an award win-
ning novelist with an immense political passion. The cover story
exposed Babangida's tactics of domination through bribery, gifts,
patronage, deceit and elimination of his political enemies. Using
Niccolo Machiavelli's *The Prince* as a theoretical compass, it
analysed the psyche of a leader who wrote the rules of the
game to suit a perennial reinvention of himself. Since no dictator likes to be anticipated, exposed and ridiculed, Babangida
raged furiously against that story.

We shared Obasa's annoyance. We, who had spent a lot of
money to make our office cosy, were forced to go underground
to practise what is now popularly called *guerrilla journalism*.
We were not going to allow the regime of Babangida to crush us.
But it was set to be a fight between David and Goliath, for 1993
was a year of draconian decrees against critical publishing and
defiant civil society. It was as if the self- styled military president
wanted a plain field on which to ride roughshod over Nigerians,
who were simply fed up with his rule.

Since our office was closed towards the end of the month,
the major problem was how our undercapitalised company
would pay the salaries of its workers. The second major problem was how to get the entire staff to remain very alert and
continue to be part of the struggle. The following Monday, we
called a meeting at the office of Sani Kabir, one of our Directors, to solve the second problem. We assured our staff that we
were going to go on because the closure and occupation of our
office was illegal. It was a threat to our livelihood: we had no
other ways of earning a living.

Although we assured the staff that we were going to go on,
we did not know the form the journey would take. But the
response to that mobilisation was spontaneous. We found that

our staff shared our courage and doggedness. Yet, just like us, these were staff who had come to join us not knowing exactly what they were in for. I speak of Timothy Bonett, Ayo Arowolo, Gbile Oshadipe, Ike Okonta, Wahab Gbadamosi, Ebenezer Obadare, Laolu Akande, Seidi Mulero, Okafor Ofiebor, Jenkins Alumona, Akin Adesokan, Muyiwa Adekeye, Ben Eguzozie, Simidele Awosika, Susan Bassey, Bagauda Kaltho, Babajide Otitoju, Sunday Dare, Grace Awodu, Yinka Tella, Ralph Ugbolu, Monday Emoni, Mudashiru Atanda, Bayo Fashoyin, the Jacob Inegbedions, the Sola Adubikas, the Peju Sanis, the Shola Aderiyes, the Adedeji Beecrofts and the Iskilu Ademuyiwas.

We just had about a hundred thousand naira in Diamondbank. We then opened an account with a name different from the one known to the government. We quickly transferred all our money into the account and informed our distributors and sales officers to ensure that payment for our products was made into that new account. We did not want Babangida to freeze our account as he did to *Newswatch* in 1987 for six months because the weekly magazine published the Cookey Political Bureau report before the government could tinker with it.

It is the nature of our industry that distributors pay you for the previous edition only when they take the current one: print media products are given to distributors on credit. It is a lopsided arrangement, which allows distributors not to return the money of the copies they collected before proscription. We met the industry in that shape. But, because of the circumstance imposed on us, we had to change it. We got some agents to pay in advance for the products. That was how we were able to pay salaries at the end of the month.

That gave everyone a boost. Even those who might have had some doubt simply said *if we get paid and we enjoy what we are doing, why don't we just continue doing it*? The risk was great, but our staff discounted it. Their disgust over the action of the junta, which ignored a Lagos High Court order to leave our office, was palpable. The staff became a source of inspiration to us.

In the meantime, the transition-to-democracy-programme for which Babangida had reportedly spent close to 40 billion naira had crumbled. The sharks within the military were about to devour themselves. Many of the politicians in the Social Democratic Party (SDP) and the National Republican Convention (NRC) were jostling to surrender to Babangida.

We reported the political events of those giddy days as if we were producing in the comfort of our offices. We were the first to publish the comprehensive results of the June 12 presidential election, which showed that M.K.O. Abiola of the SDP was the winner. We followed that up with an insider's story of the big conspiracy to abort that election and the democractic rights of Nigerians. We had reported then that General Joshua Dogonyaro, Brigadier- Generals David Mark, Anthony Ukpo, John Shagaya and Halilu Akilu were the major officers goading Babangida to cancel the presidential election.

The most popular of our editions from the underground was the special interview with General Muhammadu Buhari in which he offered a scathing criticism of the incumbent dictator. When the vendors were selling that edition secretly all over Nigeria, some security men went to the house of one of my colleagues, Dapo Olorunyomi, and harassed Ladi, his wife, who was then nursing a baby*. My own seemingly odd choice to live in Ibadan and work in Lagos at that time began to make some sense.

We kept at it for a few weeks before Babangida brought out a backdated decree with which he proscribed *TheNEWS*. We ignored it. That defiance was meant to counter the regime's

---

* Because Olorunyomi led the team that interviewed Buhari

defiance of the law. But then, Babangida's soldiers started beating up our vendors; they started arresting distributors for selling an illegal publication; they started seizing thousands of copies of *TheNEWS* from distribution vans. The five founding editors, Bayo Onanuga, Dapo Olorunyomi, Babafemi Ojudu, Seye Kehinde and myself were declared wanted on the network news of state-controlled radio and television stations. Our correspondent in Abuja, Yinka Tella, was detained. At this point, we felt that it was not fair that people should suffer so much on account of *TheNEWS*.

We decided in July 1993 to sneak into the market with a new publication. *TEMPO,* which was initially conceived as a soft sell weekly, was now born to carry on the mandate of *TheNEWS*. Because we wanted the market to know that it was just a change of name, the very first edition of *TEMPO* was exactly the same in terms of content and form as *TheNEWS*: A4 size, glossy cover and so on. We had just completed the tedious production process when some fully armed soldiers came to cart away every copy. It was a very humiliating experience. We did not cry but there was bitterness in our hearts against the bandits who were some of the people running the affairs of our country. We resolved to fight to the very end. It was one of those moments when we were not sure we would win, but we were just sufficiently motivated by ideals, which we thought would make our country outlast hopelessness.

We had one of our strategy meetings that night, but we really could not arrive at anything except a foggy idea of publishing books, or bulletins, or pamphlets of facts, periodically. There was so much outrage. We had been courageous for six weeks. Our attempt at decoy had been defeated. But by the following morning the idea of *TEMPO* in tabloid form came up. We thought it would have the advantage of being produced with speed. We were not going to allow that edition that had been seized to die. So we went ahead and reproduced it in tabloid form. It was so successful that there were no returns.

When they locked up our computers they thought that they had paralysed us. They underestimated the goodwill of so many Nigerians, who encouraged us by buying the magazine. Those of them who were working for government fed us official information. It was a very empowering factor because the same people gave us information whenever the state security was set to unleash its terror on us. One of our friends, Gbenga Fagbami, allowed us to use his business centre as a production point. Nobody would expect that we, who were being hunted, would go to Bamgbose in Lagos Island (close to the former State House at Dodan Barracks) and do our job right under their noses. Some of my colleagues still repeatedly describe the place as 'that bunker in Isale Eko!'* It was a very strategic place to use.

We identified those staff that needed to be involved in the aspect of production. We split the production into two major units: the typesetting and the printing. We limited access to the computers to very trusted typesetters. We asked the rest to go on leave. What it meant was that those who were chosen, like Jacob Inegbedion, had to work extra hours. Once you entered the place you did not leave until production was over. Staff who had nothing to do with computer production did not even know the location. Only those senior persons who needed to be involved at the point of editing were allowed to know the location. We broke into cells. There was another location where editorial people met. That place was given to us by Kehinde's brother. There was really no need for the entire editorial staff to meet together any longer. If you were a desk head you also

---

* A Lagos suburb.

belonged to a group of desk heads that would meet: only your reporters had access to you. You only met with other desk heads to put the stories together. We ensured that we had no situation where more than four or five persons were together at a particular place at the same time. We had a link person who was doing the dispatch.

As for the printing, we simply turned our sales staff into a production crew. No reporters knew the place except the founding editors. This was the aspect that the junta mythologised. All those times it was said that we were printing at the American Embassy or Cotonou, it was Alhaji Lateef Kayode Jakande, the former President of International Press Institute (IPI) and the first Executive Governor of Lagos State, who was printing for us. He was touched by our audacity*. But he was not doing it within his own premises at John West House on Acme Road, Agidingbi. He had a secret location where he had another press. The Security could not locate the place. When it was no longer safe to stay in Jakande's place, we moved over to Chief Jim Nwobodo's Satellite Press, which was then located in Lagos.

Having broken into cells, the founding editors met several times in Gbile Oshadipe's house in a suburb of Lagos before we shifted our base to Bamgbose. We discouraged visitors. It was not possible for us to have visitors. We simply went out of circulation. Obasa turned half of his flat into an administrative office. There were two long tables and chairs around them in a conference fashion and the staff continued as if nothing had happened. Obasa also turned part of his mother's house into a store. I asked him why he chose to do that. He said that it was imperative that we continued to operate. Since we had agreed to break into cells, it was important to use the most unlikely places. One of the most unlikely places when you are being hunted is

---

* His first consideration was not money, he felt that what we were doing was correct.

the place where the enemy would not expect you to be. For Obasa the last place that anybody would think he would keep the administrative, sales and account staff that were under his supervision as the General Manager, was his house and that of his mother. Obasa reckoned that nobody would question that. 'Why would an old woman be the storekeeper of *TEMPO*? You know, it was very unlikely to expect the old woman to understand what we were doing, not to talk of being an active part of it.'

Obasa however observed that we were not caught because of the goodwill of his neighbours who must have noticed our clandestine movements, but chose not to turn us in.

Tensions in the country were so high that any spark could have set off a big explosion of protest. Babangida, a short man with a super-size ego, had annulled the election on June 23, 1993. He had actually tried to stop it through the Francis Arthur Nzeribe's Association for Better Nigeria (ABN)*. Nduka Irabor, Press Secretary to the Chief of General Staff, Admiral Augustus Aikhomu, distributed the unsigned press release that voided the election to journalists in Abuja that morning. The annulment was first announced in the foreign media before it was aired on Radio Kaduna and the Network Service of the Federal Radio Corporation of Nigeria (FRCN). The unsigned release explained that the election was annulled 'to protect our legal system and the judiciary from being ridiculed and politi-cised both nationally and internationally.' It was a great insult to all those who knew that Babangida had engineered the judicial anarchy that followed the election. He had never wanted a peaceful election. One pointer to that was the ultimatum to get out of the country within 48 hours, which he gave Michael

---

* A faceless organisation apparently sponsored by the government for propaganda purposes.

O'Brien, Director of the United States Information Service, for saying on June 11, 1993 that 'any postponement of the election would cause grave concern to the US Government.'

The country, particularly the South West, erupted in anger. Many people took to the streets in protest. The soldiers mowed down about four hundred protesters in Lagos alone. The more people the soldiers killed, the more defiant the people became. Many Nigerians were now afraid that there would be another civil war. For that reason, a lot of them travelled to their home states in panic. Many died on the way. Using the Nigerian Television Authority (NTA) and the FRCN as effective propaganda tools, Uche Chukwumerije, Secretary of Information, drummed up war beats in a way that reminded Nigeria that he had been a propagandist in the Republic of Biafra during the Nigerian civil war between 1967-1970. In that climate of uncertainties, *TEMPO* was a dependable source of information. The regime, which was now under pressure, started another round of manhunt for the journalists on that magazine.

It got to a point that vendors were scared to collect *TEMPO*. We had to mobilise our staff, friends and family members to sell the magazine on the streets for three weeks. The state security was confused: vendors were not selling *TEMPO* but somehow people were getting hold of the magazine. We had people take copies to their offices and sell. Femi Falana, a famous lawyer and human rights activist, collected and sold copies through his office just because he did not want the dream to die. Adeolu Ademoyo, a university teacher, always came from Ile-Ife to collect copies for sale. There were other concerned professionals who also rose to the challenge of selling the magazine. We created alternative routes of distribution. We needed to do that because it was expedient—we did not want the enemy to defeat us. Eventually, the vendors themselves found the courage to resume sales. They collected the paper at agreed drop points in the night.

Babangida was smart enough to know the limits of his own chicanery. He 'abdicated the throne' on August 27, 1993 because of a security report that he was about to be abducted and assassinated by some officers he had thought were his allies. When Babangida addressed the joint session of the Senate and the House of Representatives on August 17, 1993, which was his birthday, he had thought that the politicians would pass a vote of confidence in him and then ask him to carry on. But that did not work out. He said, among other things: 'Following lengthy deliberations with my service chiefs, I offered as my own personal sacrifice to voluntarily *step aside* as the President and Commander-in-Chief of the Armed Forces of the Federal Republic of Nigeria.' It was the limit of hubris that he considered it a personal sacrifice to relinquish power after eight years in government. Before he 'stepped aside', he retired all other service chiefs except Abacha, who was made Secretary of Defence, in the Chief Ernest Shonekan-led Interim National Government (ING) which he inaugurated on August 26, 1993.

Our company's frosty relationship with Babangida went back to our days in the Concord Press of Nigeria Limited (CPNL). In 1992, he shut down the entire premises of the company because of a story published in the April 13 edition of *African Concord.* The story under the title 'Has IBB Given Up?' was anchored by Olorunyomi. It was a trenchant criticism of the economic and political mismanagement of the regime. It was one of the paradoxes of that time that the peg of the story was the rare interview the gap-toothed military president granted the *Sunday Times*, a paper in which the Federal Government had a controlling share. In that interview, thanks to the liberal outlook of that paper when Dr. Yemi Ogunbiyi was the Managing Director, the General admitted that his regime was incapable of fixing the economy. It was a very unpopular thing to say to the people who were expecting a positive change in an economy that had impoverished them; an economy that depended on the prescriptions which were harsher than the ones packaged in the International Monetary Fund's Structural Adjustment Programme. The cover story, which contained a biting piece by Williams entitled 'The Game is Up', and a critical interview by one of the old frontline nationalists, Mokwugo Okoye, annoyed Babangida considerably. He banned the magazine.

All the appeals of Abiola, the publisher of the magazine and Babangida's friend, fell on deaf ears. The president was too angry to see him, and Abiola began to count his losses. After a frustrating wait, the government started talking to Abiola through Colonel Halilu Akilu, the Director of the Directorate of Military Intelligence (DMI). The condition for lifting the siege was unambiguous: *go and bring a letter of apology for what African Concord has done.* So Abiola met with Onanuga, the editor of the magazine, on April 18, 1992. He told Onanuga to go and write a letter of apology to the president for the discomfort he had caused him and members of his family, the letter should say that he, Onanuga, demonstrated professional misjudgment for publishing that story. Abiola said he should bring the letter the following day and together they would go to Akilu's house with his son, Deji Abiola, who was in charge of *African Concord.* He told Onanuga that as soon as the government reopened Concord, he would sack Ojudu, one of his assistant editors, who had gone to court to contest the closure. 'It was clear from everything he said that there was no way I could stay at Concord. I knew I would not do what he asked me to do,'

Onanuga recalled.

So he consulted some senior professional colleagues who said that he should not do what Abiola asked of him. 'On April 21, 1992', Onanuga remembered, 'I wrote my resignation letter and delivered copies to the Nigerian press partly because of what Abiola said to me about a regime that was capable of arranging accidents and partly because the public deserved to know what was happening to *African Concord*.'

I also resigned the following day. So did Olorunyomi, Ojudu and Kehinde. We did not resign because we had any other media house in mind. We did not resign because we had money in our bank accounts. As a matter of fact, because our April salary was not paid, we had to make do with token allowances given to us by the Nigeria Union of Journalists, Lagos Chapel, which Lanre Arogundade led. Babangida had set the house ablaze. We were now out in the cold.

One of the points Onanuga made in his letter of resignation was that 'Journalism is not meant to make the environment cosy for leaders of nations; it is to prod them to act in the interest of the larger society: it is meant to cause them sleepless nights'. Abiola's response was that he did not set up his conglomerate to give anybody sleepless nights. On one of those cold days, I looked in on Onanuga in his house and asked him to reconcile his position with that of Abiola. Onanuga explained that 'the press is called the fourth estate of the realm and it is at par with the other estates, each of which has its own role in society. In our case, we're called the watchdogs, or even the guard dogs, or the bridge between the rulers and the ruled. We should not only mirror what the government is doing, but also the feelings of the people, particularly in an environment where you don't have a viable opposition, where you don't have genuine democratic structures. The press should be there to play the role of a responsible opposition party. Once the press abdicates that responsibility, there would be problems. The leaders would be operating without constraints. When I say the press should give leaders sleepless nights, it is in that context. I believe every bad leader should be afraid of opening the papers every morning.'

There was no reconciliation yet. Which was why I further prodded him: *You don't think that your position contradicts the objectives of Abiola in setting up his press*? 'Not at all', he said. 'Abiola set up that press to achieve what he called harmony in the society. How do you achieve harmony in a society where the public is clearly antagonistic towards its government or where the regime is carrying out so many anti- people policies? That's discord, and the press should mirror the attendant tension. There are fundamental disagreements in Nigerian society between the government and the public interest. The press should try to resolve the contradictions to create harmony. In *African Concord,* we tried to achieve a kind of harmony between the publisher's interest and the public interest. The interest of the two must merge, otherwise the magazine wouldn't have sold the way it did. There was a *Morning Post* in Nigeria set up by the government. It followed rigidly the dictum: he who pays the piper dictates the tune. It died. And look at *New Nigerian*. It used to be a credible paper until some sycophants took over the running of it. Now, that paper is a shadow of its former self.'

Whenever the history of the Concord Press Nigeria Limited is written, it would have to take account of its several phases. Founded on March 1, 1980, when Abiola was a staunch member of the National Party of Nigeria (NPN), the titles in the stable were rabidly anti- Obafemi Awolowo, the leader of the Unity Party of Nigeria (UPN), who was also using his own paper, *Nigerian Tribune*, which he founded on November 19,

1949, to fight all his political opponents. When Abiola resigned his membership of the NPN in 1982 because the party on which he had spent a huge amount of money would not nominate him as a presidential candidate, the editorial direction of his press also changed.

Since Abiola was no longer in partisan politics, his journalists were able to report with some measure of objectivity. The sales figure rose to an all-time high. This was when Dele Giwa, Ray Ekpu, Yakubu Mohammed, Doyin Abiola, Duro Onabule, Tom Borha, Sina Adedipe, Lewis Obi, Nosa Igiebor, Dare Babarinsa, Dimgba Igwe, Mike Awoyinfa, Dele Omotunde and several others actually became well known to the reading public. It was a flowering phase. Journalism was, at this point, on its way to achieving great goals, in part because it was free, and in part because it was backed by enormous resources. Abiola reaped the benefits abundantly. Nigeria and the world toasted him as a powerful publisher. He earned some political influence, which all his other business ventures could not have bought. It was typical of him at that time to exaggerate his influence because of the reach and power of his press. With the exit of Giwa and others (who left to establish *Newswatch* in 1985), Concord experienced what I like to call *comme ci, comme ca* phase. It was not as much of an ebb in sales as that of a strength of character, a strength of vision.

When we took over *African Concord* in 1989, we filled a vacuum that seemed long in waiting with a very critical phase. Onanuga headed a crew of talented and self-motivated workers which included Ohi Alegbe, Seyi Olu Awofeso, Rita Edah, Demola Oguntayo, Bosah Iwobi, Jon Offei Ansah, Victor Omuabor, Demola Abimboye, Doyin Iyiola, Jide Fatogun, Obiora Chukwumba, Timothy Bonnet, Babatunde Olugboji, Femi Macaulay and Dokun Abioye, the brilliant cartoonist who unfortunately died in an autocrash. Although Sam Omatseye and Tunji Bello were on the political desk of *National Concord,* they wrote constantly for the magazine because they shared our political temperament. Patrick Wilmot, the Ahmadu Bello University radical intellectual, who was hounded out of Nigeria by Babangida, wrote every week for the magazine under a pseudonym, Ahmed Abdullahi. Lewis Obi, our unassuming Editor-in-Chief, who also wrote elegantly every week, was a solid backstage motivator and a moderating influence.

As soon as we took over, Babangida dissolved his cabinet. While other magazines focussed on the reshuffle, we did a story on General Domkat Bali, the Minister of Defence and Chairman Joint Chiefs of Staff. He had been made Minister of Internal Affairs, a position just vacated by an officer, Brigadier John Shagaya, who was junior to him. We called it *The Fall of Bali.* Using people as pegs to analyse issues was to be a distinctive feature of that very critical phase. The very day that magazine hit the streets, Babangida announced the resignation of Bali. From that moment on, we were marked by the government. The critics of the government felt comfortable speaking to the magazine even though we relayed the government's view of issues as well. We yielded our cover pages to Great Ogboru and other prime movers of the Major Gideon Gwarza Orka coup of April 22, 1990. When William Keeling, a journalist with *Financial Times* of London, was deported for writing a story on how the windfall from the Gulf War was squandered, we spoke with him in London and put him on the cover because of the weight of what he knew and had to say.

We questioned the sincerity of Babangida's promises to leave office when he created new states and local governments. It was a legitimate story because it's our duty as journalists to raise questions. Babangida had to appeal to the people to have faith in him. We came out the following week on why people did not have any trust in his government. It was because of Babangida's over-manipulation of the system that he became known rather derisively as Maradona (after an ace Argentine footballer, Diego Maradona, who allegedly scored a controversial goal in a crucial match, without following the rules of the game). For the first time since we took over, Abiola asked us to soft pedal. He said we should not be seen to be going all out to attack the government. We backed off for some time in deference to him until the *Atkins adverts* came out, campaigning, in conjunction with Akani Aluko's *Third Eye* pullout in *Sunday Tribune*, that Babangida must prolong his stay in office. In March 1992, things were so bad for Nigerians that a lot of people thought it was going to be the end of the country. We had to do our job: a comprehensive story on the state of the nation, which incurred the wrath of the dictator. He sealed off the press.

Not too long after the mass resignation from *African Concord*, some of us were invited to join *The African Guardian,* which Sully Abu had just been assigned to manage. It was great working with Abu. For the short period that we were on the magazine, many readers noticed that we affected the life of *The African Guardian* positively. I remember that one of the early stories we did was a critical one on the National Guard which Babangida established in May 1992 because of the unending crises of riots, bloody carnage and severe fuel shortages, which were obvious signals of his loss of authority. 'Henceforth, all incidents of civil unrest will be dealt with using all means, including the use of emergency powers'. That was the language of force with which Babangida heralded the National Guard. The Guard would soon become a tunnel through which money was siphoned from the national treasury.

On November 17, 1993, Abacha sacked the interim government of Shonekan, which a Lagos High Court had, in any case, declared illegal. In his first broadcast, which I heard on Odia Ofeimun's car radio, on November 18, 1993, Abacha lied to the nation that Shonekan resigned voluntarily, but *TEMPO* insisted that it was a coup. From his first week in office we had indicated that we would constantly touch on his raw nerves even though in that broadcast he had warned that he would deal decisively with anyone who attempted 'to test our will'.

Not minding that threat, the University of Ibadan students were already at the gate of their institution to protest against the coup of Abacha when a team of armed policemen came to disperse them. Ofeimun, Harry Garuba and myself were among the crowd of people opposite the gate. I remember that the leader of the team came after Ofeimun and gave him two slaps on the face. Some bullets flew past Garuba, the author of *Shadow and Dream,* who was lying flat on his belly on the road. It was a brutal dispersal that we never bargained for. As we headed straight for his car, Ofeimun, one of the highly gifted Nigerian poets, and an award-winning political analyst, said rather prophetically: 'This government will be very bad'.

We were no strangers to Abacha. He was a sly, sadistic Robespierre who had waited for this moment. When he was Defence Minister under Babangida, he wanted to invest in our company through his son, Ibrahim (who later died in an air crash). The money they were bringing was large and tempting, but we told him to hold the money until his father left government. Again, just before Abacha staged his coup against the ING, General Oladipo Diya, who would soon become his second-in-command, was sent to find out what our position on the national crisis was. We thought we had made ourselves clear enough in the nature of the stories we were running. We told Diya that what would solve the problem was a restoration of democracy, not another military coup. We were speaking to the deaf.

This was the period when some pro-democracy activists and many politicians, including Abiola, fell for the deceit of Abacha that he would only rule for six months to stabilise the country before Abiola would take over. Not many people knew that it was a lie until Brigadier-General David Mark, in an interview with *Newswatch* magazine in 1994, told the nation that the real plan of Abacha was to stay in power for at least five years. Mark, who lost out in the power struggle that put Abacha in power, further said that the intention to remain in power for five years was a betrayal of the hopes and aspirations of Nigerians. Abacha was furious. Top editors of *Newswatch*: Ray Ekpu, Dan Agbese and Yakubu Mohammed were rounded up and detained. Mark, too, was declared wanted.

Abacha's reign would be characterised by such deceit and incredible capacity for infinite meanness and greed, but Abiola had entered the trap before he realised it. Afterwards, he tried to fight back, declaring himself the president on the eve of the first anniversary of the annulled June 12 presidential election. He said that from that day, he had begun to run a government of national unity as the President and Commander-in-Chief and called on Abacha and members of his ruling council to resign. He also called on the people of Nigeria 'to emulate the actions of their brothers and sisters in South Africa and stand up as one person to throw away the yoke of minority rule for ever.' He naively forgot that the struggle in South Africa had had a long gestation period. By the time Abiola made that speech called *Epetedo Declaration,* the political ground beneath his feet had already shifted: many of the politicians around him had ditched him. For instance, his Vice President-Elect, Alhaji Baba Gana

ingibe, had joined the government of Abacha. Demonstrating
hat his government was in control, Abacha arrested Abiola.
He was to remain in detention until he died four years later, one
month after Abacha himself passed on.

Before Abiola claimed his mandate, we were very critical of
his apparent timidity and desultory vacillation, particularly when
he flew to London following a tip off that he was about to be
killed by some soldiers. We were annoyed with him that he still
wrote a rather friendly letter to Babangida when a lot of people
were being killed in the streets because of the annulment of the
June 12 election. Because of our unrelenting criticism of him,
Abiola actually said in a press interview that some people were
weeping more than the bereaved. We did not relent. It got to a
point that he sent Dele Alake, Segun Babatope and Tunji Bello
to us. He explained that he had been busy consulting potential
allies and that he would never abandon the struggle.

Critical journalism, then, was ahead of concerned Nigerians
from different ethnic groups who formed the National Democratic Coalition (NADECO) on May 15, 1994. The communi-
que it issued at that first meeting called on all Nigerians to boy-
cott the election into the Constitutional Conference, which the
regime of Abacha was going to hold on May 23, 1994. It said
that the conference was a ruse and called on the government to
organise a Sovereign National Conference and actualise Abiola's
mandate. When the call of NADECO was obeyed, mainly in
the South West, Abacha decided to deal ruthlessly with its members. He compulsorily retired Major-General Chris Alli, the Chief
of Army Staff and Vice-Admiral Allison Madueke, the Chief of
Naval Staff, who had been mounting pressures on him to de-
mocratise the polity. He did this in the last week of August 1994
to browbeat others, who might be critical of him. He demanded
absolute loyalty. From this moment, Major Hamza Al-

Mustapha, his Chief Security Officer, was invested with maximum power. All the officers and civilians around Diya, his deputy, were put under surveillance.

This did not dampen the spirit of NADECO members. They campaigned against almost everything that Abacha set out to do including the hosting of the Under-17 soccer tournament. In a memo it sent to the Federation of International Football Associations (FIFA) which *TheNEWS* published on March 13, 1995, NADECO observed that while Nigerians loved football and were always eager to support any national sporting event, most especially soccer, they saw that period as a time to resolve the nation's political and economic crises, not a period to revel in the hosting of a World Championship. It saw the regime's desperation to host this tournament as another attempt 'to divide and conquer Nigerians, unite our people around mere symbols rather than substance and turn the attention of the international community away from its blood-chilling record.'

The NADECO activists went on to say that hosting the two-week championship in Nigeria would drag the name of FIFA in the mud. It, therefore, urged it to choose an alternative venue, preferably in Africa, as a way of setting 'minimum standards which hosting nations must meet, not just in erecting superficial infrastructures, but also in guaranteeing the safety and security of participants.' Nigeria did not get the right to host the championship.

Because of our critical coverage of Abacha's rule, he marked our company down as one of his arch opponents, but unexpectedly flattered us by hiring hacks to produce fake copies of *TheNEWS* and *TEMPO,* along with *TELL,* the other critical magazine, with stories singing his praises. Our readers were not fooled. By vigorously probing his regime, we were merely fulfilling part of the promise that we had made at our first outing. We had resolved to dedicate ourselves to the principles of nationalism, democracy, political and economic pluralism, liberty and equality of the various ethnic groups of the Nigerian federation. In doing this, we had promised to adhere strictly to the ethics of the profession and to give our compatriots products that would be aesthetically satisfying. We set up *TheNEWS* in February 1993 to be a true people's magazine, which would breathe a fresh air of patriotism into Nigerians. We set it up to tear apart the mask of lies in our national life. Looking back now, we exposed ourselves to grave dangers, considering that those who were murdered by the regimes of Babangida and Abacha were no greater nuisances to those regimes than we were.

For simply being a factor in the resistance, I was *jailed for life*. That episode in my life was like a push off a cliff. How did I survive? I call upon the recent past to explain.

TWO

The Wiles
of Vultures

'**M**anagement meeting fixed for 1700hrs at *TheNEWS* office. Report on time. To discuss the technical problems of *A.M. NEWS*. Urgent!'

The courier of that notice had barely left when I made straight for my car to attend the meeting, which was going to hold at Isheri Road. But at the front of the Nigerian Institute of Journalism (NIJ) in Ogba, there was a traffic jam on the ever-busy Ijaiye Road. Nearby, I saw Obasa in the back seat of a cream-coloured station wagon. He popped his head out of the window and sent me a coded message: *they are here*.

I knew instantly that we were in some kind of trouble with the State. Why were we being hunted again? Was this the beginning of the promised clampdown? Which member of the Nigerian Intelligence Community had come for us? Was it the Defence Agency? Could it be the National Intelligence Agency? Or the State Security Service? Could it be the Directorate of Military Intelligence? Or the Criminal Investigation Department of the Force Headquarters? Was it the newly created BodyGuards to Ibrahim, the son of the Head of State? Or the

Federal Investigation and Intelligence Bureau? All of these security outfits could arrest you for any reason under Abacha.

As I drove on, I perspired profusely, not merely as a result
of the heat and high humidity of the Lagos weather at that time
of the year. Having gone through the closure of *TheNEWS* in
1993, and experienced the problems of fighting back for months
with *TEMPO* from the underground, virtually all the old hands
in the organisation knew what to do whenever it was time to
operate invisibly. I was apprehensive about *A.M. NEWS*, a new
daily, which we established on April 3, 1995. Could we afford
to practise *guerrilla journalism* with it? It was not quite clear
to me that the support of the entire crew could be guaranteed
every inch of the way.

I was now at a safe location where I could see *TheNEWS*
offices very clearly. There were no soldiers or policemen in
sight. I parked the car, looked again at the surroundings of the
offices, to be sure, then entered the building. Onanuga,
Olorunyomi, Ojudu and Kehinde, were anxiously awaiting me.
As soon as I entered the newsroom, I was told that the operatives of the SSS had come for me.

This was May 22, 1995.

I was being invited for a chat with the SSS in connection
with the cover story of *TheNEWS* of that week written by
Babajide Otitoju: *Not Guilty—Army Panel Clears Coup Suspects*. That story had relied heavily on the preliminary report of
the Special Investigation Panel (SIP) headed by Brigadier–
General Felix Mujakperuo. In that report, the panel had said
that all the officers who were initially brought before it as coup
suspects were not guilty of the offence. But the Head of State
thought differently. He was desperate to find the officers and
civilians guilty and condemned, just to purge the country of
political rivals and potential critics—a necessary first step towards dictatorship.

Bereft of courage to stick to the truth and damn the conse-
quences, Mujakperuo and his men promptly commenced a meticulous search in late March 1995 for more coup suspects. It
was not just because they did not want to incur the lunatic fury
of the Head of State; the bonus they would get after that crucial
assignment was just as important. The first major symptom of a
regime going irretrievably murderous had started manifesting
itself, but the unwary nation was yet to notice.

The magazine did not only tell this story; it went further to say
that the assault on some of the most brilliant officers arrested
was a truly terrifying drama that should be halted without delay.
What we did was not a risky story lacking in facts even though
there was a minor error of fact in it (Major-General Rufus
Kupolati never headed any investigation panel before that of
Mujakperuo as the magazine claimed). We knew that the story
was capable of enraging the ruling junta because it set off a
national alarm. But we did not know that it could provoke the
regime of Abacha into placing us on a long list of imaginary
coup plotters. The cover story would soon serve as a basis for
which I was tried and imprisoned.

Yet I was not the one who edited that story. I was not even
present at the editorial meeting that decided quite rightly to run
it as the lead. In fact, I had ceased to be the editor of *TheNEWS*
from January 1995, having been given a new assignment by the
Management Committee: to put together a vibrant Editorial
Board for our new daily, *A.M.NEWS*. A high-energy assignment, which was difficult to combine with the brain-racking job
of editing a weekly like *TheNEWS*. Olorunyomi was given the
duty of running the magazine, and part of his task was the re-
cruitment of a new editor. But The*NEWS* was still carrying my
imprint as its editor.

It would have been pointless to inundate the agents of the
SSS who had come for me with all those details. Even if my

:aptors were not so much in a hurry to go with me, I would not
lave told them because it did not matter to us who was the
:aptive. Each of us knew that official assignments could come
it anytime and in any form. We knew that betrayal would not
nake our humanity prevail. For me, therefore, the SSS warrant
vas a summons, asking me to lift up the burden of truth: to carry
he banner of the organisation with tenderness. If I had failed to
lo that I would have let down my associates.

The operatives were waiting.

Should I go with them right away, knowing that I could be-
:ome a victim of some highly placed but unbelievably treacher-
)us fellows; characters who maim others, and in turn mangle
Vigeria, in a bid for political power?

I felt calm, but I was hungry. I turned to the officer in charge
)f the State agents, pleading with him to let me eat before they
ook me away. He refused.

The weather was downcast.

I was telling Olorunyomi to inform Bunmi (my wife) of my
irrest and to help me proof-read and send the letters I had
vritten to some of the special contributors to *A.M. NEWS,* when
he leader of the SSS gang cut me short and led me to the
vaiting car. The engine turned impatiently and we hit the road to
>hangisha, a Lagos suburb. Travelling this way naturally re-
ninded me of the activists who had been dragged along its
larkling path. They had come back with tales of pains. *What
tories would I bring from this curve, this road that leads to
mguish?*

[t was not the first time that year that someone from my or-
L ganisation would be invited to the office of the SSS located in
>hangisha. Indeed, the operative who effected my arrest, had
:d a different team to our office earlier in the year when *TEMPO*

ran a report by two of its correspondents, Remi Oyeyemi and Ben Eguzozie, on the meningitis outbreak in Ibadan and Calabar at a time that FIFA inspection team was in the country. The government, which had wanted to use the hosting of the Under-17 soccer fiesta to shore up its muddied image, both at home and abroad, had spent so much money to paper over the stench in our hospitals and the very bad conditions of our stadia and hotels. We are a soccer-crazy nation and every government knows that football could seduce our people to rally round the flag.

As soon as it was clear that Nigeria was not going to be given the right to host the fiesta, following the statement from FIFA's president, Joao Havelange, asking Nigeria to put its request to host the championship on hold, the peevish officials in Abuja, the nation's political capital, thought that the story had something to do with it. Onanuga was arrested for that reason. After some days, the SSS sent him to the Federal Investigation and Intelligence Bureau (FIIB), Alagbon Close, Lagos, for further questioning. As it turned out, the objects of their attention were so laughable: the films of the story that *TEMPO* had published.

The regime was obviously angry with us for helping FIFA to take its own carefully considered decision!

The same SSS man who arrested me had led the team that arrested Chido Onumah over a story in *A.M.NEWS* of how a con man duped Diya. The veracity of the story was not contested; the operatives who grilled the reporter were simply interested in his reason for running the story. Onumah spent more than a week in Shangisha.

Doifie Ola and Alex Kabba had, in 1994, suffered arrest and detention in police cells for different stories: the former for reporting the case of Abacha's bribe to some judges and the latter for his story on how Aminu Saleh, the Secretary to the

Government of the Federation (SGF) under Abacha improperly acquired land in Abuja already allocated to other Nigerians. When he told his cellmates that he worked for *TEMPO,* they treated him with respect.

My colleagues had dispersed after the management meeting, hoping that I would be let off after a week or so. But I was allowed to go home that very night. What happened? The SSS officials took a risk. When we got to their office very close to 7:00 PM, another official duty was going on: Falana was being quizzed. They wanted to know, among other things, why he had elected to defend Ken Saro-Wiwa and other Ogoni leaders, who were then in detention over an alleged murder case. As an advocate of democracy, Falana had been a victim of repeated arbitrary arrests and detentions by military regimes in Nigeria. To wait for my own turn, the officials ordered that I be locked up in one of the offices. I whiled away the time just trying to read the advance copy of *A.M.NEWS*, but I could not concentrate.

When they came to attend to me around 9:30PM, they seemed dog-tired, but they assigned one of their men to interrogate me. The black-suited operative, who was in his late forties, sat down and motioned me to the seat in front of him. He then pointed his forefinger at the copy of *TheNEWS* of that week on his table and began a dialogue which was something of this nature:

'Tell me', he asked, 'why have you people published a terrible story like this?'

I stared at him for a second or two.

'Why?' he said.

'Why not?' I answered.

We exchanged glances. The man was visibly offended by my informality.

I continued, 'you should tell me why you consider a harmless story terrible. What is terrible about it?'

The black-suited man had read the story and was now ready to delve into it, but his eyes once again caught the headline. He stopped from opening the magazine right away and asked, 'Do you know that the suspects you people are claiming have been cleared are still in military custody?'

He looked a bit relaxed.

'Yes, we know they are still in detention. But that's not fair.'

'Oh, you know they are still being detained. If the military has cleared them, do you think the same military will still continue to hold them?'

I paused a moment. The man scrutinised me. I then said, 'That's for the military to sort out.'

'You've not answered my question.'

Another pause. He folded his arms on his chest.

'Okay, let's put it this way: An agent of the government may do something today and the principal may decide to overrule it tomorrow. What you have in the interval is confusion, that only those who are causing it can explain.'

'We don't have time to waste', he grumbled.

He then lit a cigarette.

'You have published a lie.' His voice was rising now, as his tone became truculent.

'No self-respecting newspaper or magazine will trade in falsehoods', I replied. 'As I said at the beginning, the onus is on you to prove that we have goofed. What, if I may ask, is the true story?'

'Was the writer a member of the panel? How did he know what the panel decided?' My interrogator asked.

The smoke was gathering in the room now and the man watched its forming spirals. I pressed myself against the backrest of the chair as I responded, 'You and I know that the writer doesn't have to be a member of the panel to write about its decision. It is simple, isn't it?'

'I see. You people just sit down in your office and concoct stories.'

'It is great to listen to the other side, but isn't it simply impossible to do so all the time?'

'I am telling you that this story is false. No panel has cleared any officer. Whoever has told you this lie is a rogue. You hear me. The informant must be a rogue. You too should be ashamed of yourself, instead of sitting here defending this trash...'

The shrill voice was as startling as it was encrusted with anger. I wasn't moved by his tantrums. What story had I defended? The operative leaned back against his own seat — waiting for what? My reply? *Why should I continue to converse with a man who was only interested in hearing his own voice?*

Silence.

I was beginning to get angry. It's part of my nature that I can't hide my feelings. Not that I cannot contain myself— in fact, some of my acquaintances consider me mild tempered. The man noticed my countenance and was very pleased with the result of his effort. He drew the magazine closer to himself and was about to open it when I said, 'This whole business will come to nothing if we continue like this. Since this *chat* started I have extended to you all the respect that your office deserves. It has been abuse all the way from your side.'

The black-suited man ignored me and continued.

'You people should have known that this is a sensitive matter. I can't understand Nigerian journalists. Why are you so reckless? Read this sentence. Read it. This is libellous. You don't have to do that, do you? You don't even have respect for our traditional rulers. You call them 'wayfaring royals'.

As far as I was concerned, what he described as defamatory was just a mildly critical sentence. I offered a harmless reply. A joke, actually.

'Is the Head of State not a man like us? I understand he wakes up at 11.00 AM almost everyday, goes to the office at 1:00 PM and leaves at 3:00 PM for the club to unwind'.

The evening had gone, leaving us with a dark night in Shangisha. It was getting quite cold. He lit another cigarette. I could not hold my breath for much longer. I felt the sting of his smoke in my nostrils. At first glance, one might be tempted to think that he was engaged in some kind of tiring job. Not really. He was just irritated. I had uttered a blasphemy before a fanatical acolyte of a god. He looked at me worriedly, perhaps debating in some region of his mind whether or not to settle the score once and for all with a killer punch. Eventually, good sense prevailed, giving birth to a sudden, vehement spitting, just like the spraying attack of a cobra that has turned round on its pursuers.

'You're a foolish man. You're ill-mannered. The Head of State is old enough to be your father and should be treated with due respect. Even if you don't respect him, what of his office? I can't understand what the press has become. A licence to soil people's reputation? Reputation which people have built over the years will be ruined by one article. Is that journalism? You don't know you're in for serious trouble. You don't know…'

The black-suited operative had not said anything tangible about the cover story. So I said to myself: *calm down, don't bandy words with a fool. Your silence is enough: ignore him. His tirade, anyway, is directed at the gutter press, which you also dislike. Save your breath. Better to let his idiocy pass. It is so crazy, is it not, how people who know nothing about journalism have become its most outspoken critics?* It was laughable to see him attempt to pass vacuous pronouncements as legitimate criticism. But the threat, which his reproach contained, I did not take lightly.

'Before you kill me, you should at least let me know what I am being accused of…'

Just then there was a knock on the door. An individual bounced in and asked, 'How far?'

The black-suited agent, the hurler of insults, reported to the intruder the shape the encounter had taken. It appeared to be a fairly comprehensive report. He took another drag on his cigarette, eyed me and exhaled slowly. The newcomer turned to me, going by his initial desperate and indignant look, I was expecting a more abrasive language. Instead, what he said baffled me.

'How do you do?' he asked.

I nodded slightly. Plus a shrug. He read indifference on my face.

'I don't expect you to feel bad about everything that has happened here tonight. We're just doing our job. There is no problem at all. You will be going home, soon. But you will need to report back tomorrow morning to see our boss, and it will be *all over*. I will personally take you to your house now.'

Since it was after 10:00 PM, I had already braced myself up for detention that night, but the red road of my inexorable destiny, the sinister labyrinths of my march to captivity, were being given a facelift. I was simply being asked to tarry awhile before I embarked on a trip into an uncertain future. My dream would soon dissolve into a nightmare.

In an instant, we reached the Lagos-Ibadan Express Way, crossed over to the side of 7-Up plant and then Billings Way. I explained to him that I could find my way home from Ikeja bus stop, but when we got to Lateef Jakande Road in Agidingbi, I changed my mind and came down at the first bus stop, opposite Coca-Cola plant. I took a cab to the office.

Onanuga, whom I met there, suggested I should not go back to Shangisha the next day, after I had told him the story of my 'chat' with the SSS chaps. But some of my other colleagues were not so apprehensive. I also felt that we should honour our pledge. The persuasive argument was that we were not an illegal organisation, and we should stop treating ourselves as such. We did not have any inkling of the sort of regime we were dealing with. We never suspected that the SSS was an extension of the dragnet to catch 'coup plotters'.

B elieving that it was going to be just another passing show of arrogant power, I breezed into the office of the SSS by 10:00AM. the following day. I was kept waiting for more than four hours in their big reception hall. Waiting and waiting. It was quite exhausting, this endless waiting for the big boss. I was already slipping into sleep (it was just impossible to resist the drowsy attack for I stayed the night in the office) when the smooth intruder of the previous day came calling.

'Oh, sorry: we've kept you waiting for so long. I'm very sorry. Let me see...emm...', glancing at his wrist watch now, 'I've arranged for you to go and meet our boss at our Ikoyi office, he will talk to you.'

It was a lie. He was not sending me to Ikoyi; he was sending me, without a road map, to a dreaded place.

The car was waiting.

I was squeezed between two snoopers. Mum was the word in the car as we headed straight for Ketu and meandered through the area before we finally hit Mile 12 Expressway, facing Ojota. After the engine had cleared its throat, the car raced through Maryland, Anthony, Palmgrove, Ojuelegba, Western Avenue and Costain. I noticed that the man sitting by my right had a pistol in his pocket. I felt jittery.

When I also noticed that we started heading to Apapa instead of Ikoyi, I asked, 'Where are you taking me?' They said nothing. NOTHING.

'Would you like to read these?' I passed all my morning newspapers to them. They still remained quiet.

Thoughts of contract assassins began to race through my mind. Had our country not become a den of assassins? My fear was noticeable when it occurred to me that I might just vanish. We were on Malu Road, Apapa, in a matter of minutes. It then started drizzling. I began to shiver from cold inside the ragged car, which now drove slowly. We saw two soldiers waiting by the roadside and our driver, an old man, was ordered to stop by one of my escorts. What was the problem? The gangling escort alighted very quickly from the car and pulled aside one of the soldiers. He asked some questions from him in hushed tones, but the soldier's reply was loud enough for me to hear: description of a shortcut to the Directorate of Military Intelligence (DMI).

We had obviously taken a wrong turn, so we had to change course somewhere in Ajegunle. The last time I had been to this place was for an Arts Stampede organised by the Committee for Relevant Art (CORA) at Ayota Arts Centre, a grassroots playhouse, owned by Segun Taiwo, who later died in his prime.

I beheld some kids playing in the mixture of cow-dung and human waste. I beheld also the insipid sadness on the faces of poor people—men and women who probably had run from the poverty of their villages only to jump into the trap and sprawling squalor of Ajegunle. They were a true representation of the wretched Lagosians, many of who labour sometimes with dignity from sun-up to sun-down only to end up living dangerously as they are led desperately into the embrace of a mirage.

The drizzle graduated into rain and it was in that heavy downpour that we drove to the Child Avenue headquarters of DMI .

THREE

~~~~

The Snoopers
Caged Me

The pouring rain and the rolling thunder had ceased. There were puddles all over and water was trickling out of the back of the building as a soldier led me out of the stuffy, grubby waiting room with a gun pointed at me. No promise of the sun. We entered the reception room through the Directorate's outer staircase. Waiting to receive me was the man in charge of my case: Lieutenant-Colonel Stephen Idehenre. The two of us left for his office. As soon as I was seated, two other officers stepped into the room. Idehenre declared the session open.

'I have been told that you slept in the SSS office.'

I didn't bother to contradict the lie. I only added, 'Where I was interrogated'.

'No, that's for the SSS. Regard this as your first interrogation, and it's going to be easy as long as you cooperate with us'.

Then the swarthy officer, who I was told worked in the Psychological Operations unit, asked, 'What do you think should be the role of the press in Nigeria?'

'Well, I cannot think of any other fitting role, any other responsible role for the press, than the one stipulated in the Code of Ethics for Nigerian Journalists', I answered.

'Do you think that you people have been playing that role?'

'Yes.'

'With all the lies and rumours that the press print in this country?'

I took a deep breath. It seemed to me that I had to choose my words carefully here.

'I believe that it is the role of the press to provide criticism and provoke debate rather than act as praise singers.'

The third interrogator, Lieutenant-Colonel Olaonipekun Majoyeogbe, chuckled and said that the recklessness in the media was because the so-called critical journalists were just willing tools of the politicians.

I replied that it was not a crime to be interested in politics and that we were not anybody's cronies. 'The truth of the matter is that we are neither for the politicians nor for the military—we are for the truth, we are for the public interest...'

Majoyeogbe, a fast talker, cut me short.

'And who is in the best position to know what constitutes the public interest: the government or the press?'

Since he appeared in need of it, and since I could think of worse ways of passing our enforced time together, I pressed on, 'I don't think we've had any government that has demonstrated a sophisticated understanding of the public interest. It is the responsibility of a reporter to protect the public interest against arrogant, powerful and privileged elements in society. Time and again, our company has done stories in respect of this professional precept.'

I could swear I was beginning to enjoy myself, which was something of an unexpected bonus. Then Idehenre intervened,

'Let's get down to the real business. You're here to help us with our investigation. As I said at the beginning, we need your full cooperation. As you will have observed, we are also educated; we are not simply jackboots. We don't kill people here. We're also here to safeguard the interest of the nation in the same way you people are interested in what you earlier referred to as protecting the public interest. Now, to start with, what do you think about the coup, particularly the way it is being handled by the press?'

Idehenre was trying to be clever with his general remark concerning the profile of his organisation, he seemed to want sympathy. I tried to explain, as diplomatically as I could, that it was not the press that was confusing the public on the coup issue; it was the military itself.

'How do you reconcile what Brigadier-General Fred Chijuka of the Defence Public Relations (DPR) said on the coup with what was said by the Chief of Defence Staff, General Abdulsalami Abubakar? The former said the whole thing was a rumour; that the officers arrested so far were rounded up because they were disgruntled and that they would soon be released. A few days later, Abubakar was on the network stating in strong terms, that the officers were coup suspects. Who is confusing the public? Are the officers guilty of an offence? This is the first time in the history of coup plotting in Nigeria that the military has contradicted itself in public. It's particularly scary and worrisome. Isn't it?...'

'No. no. no. Forget about what Chijuka said. He didn't know what he was talking about', Majoyeogbe interrupted me. I was a bit irritated because I knew that Chijuka based his information on the DMI's report, which stated that there hadn't been a coup.

Before I met him I had heard a story about Majoyeogbe

which left me with a feeling of contempt. In 1984, he had created a scene in Command Secondary School, Kaduna, during the Captain-to-Major examination of the Command and Staff College. Babangida, who was then the Chief of Army Staff, had turned up stealthily like a serpent at the venue. At the emergency assembly convened to welcome him, he inquired if anyone had a complaint. Majoyeogbe, then a Captain, responded by saying that he was not satisfied with the way the examination was being conducted; that there was no confidentiality in the ways the question papers were being handled, and this had led to leaks. He said, to the consternation of all present, that he had seen some of the papers with some of the candidates before the examination.

The accusation came like a bombshell. The examiners were not only embarrassed; they were also very angry that they were being publicly disgraced. Babangida promptly set up a panel of inquiry to investigate the matter. Majoyeogbe, who obtained 50% in the examination, had no witnesses. He had no evidence. The case was therefore dismissed. Was he just being used as a pawn in the intriguing chess game of a superior officer? Now I was faced with this same man trying to present Abubakar's manipulation of fact as truth.

'Whether Chijuka was right or wrong is not the issue now.' I said. 'The point is that the military is sorely divided over this case.'

'Is that a good enough reason for you to publish falsehoods?'

'What falsehoods?'

He then showed me his own copy of *TheNEWS* of that week which he had marked in so many places with red ink.

'Look, you write here that the DMI said there was no coup. That's a lie. Nobody has been cleared by any panel. If you want to see where the traitors are being kept, I can arrange it. I will give you uniform and take you there.' The dark officer from the Psychological Operations, who was not wearing a nametag, backed him up.

'Is it professional to publish falsehoods? I don't know what you stand to gain by this; I just don't know. I don't know,' he stressed.

When I observed that they were beginning to enjoy their own jeremiad, I said, 'As I told the SSS, we've not closed the chapter on the coup story. If you make your own side of this story available, we will print it next week.'

'You know that will not stop the spread of falsehoods in this country. The only way to stop it is to get rid of those who are misinforming the press'. Idehenre said, in an obvious attempt to cajole me. 'That's the only way to help you and our country. You have to tell us who gave you the story. Who is the person who wants to ruin your organisation with falsehoods?'

They knew I would hedge.

'Well, let me say that we have our own way of detecting lies', I explained. 'An example that readily comes to mind now is the cover story we ran to mark the 1993 anniversary of the bomb attack on Giwa, the Editor-in-Chief of *Newswatch*. Someone was peddling a story, saying that he knew who had assassinated the renowned journalist. We set to work. We ran to every corner of the country following his leads. After weeks of investigation, we discovered that the man was a fake. Some people wanted to use the fellow to confuse Nigerians about the identity of the real killers. While some other papers and magazines fell for the story, hook, line and sinker, we warned our readers to beware of the poison in the market. As to the source of our story, I'm afraid, I can't help you. It is against the ethics of journalism to reveal my sources just as it is against the ethics of your job and oath of office to divulge information about *top secret* operations.'

There was a long pause. My interrogators looked at one another and then at me. They said nothing. Deadlock? They lingered over their choices as the man from the Psychological Operations unit left the room, followed shortly by Majoyeogbe. It was 5:40 PM. They left without farewell. *Were they going to subject me to torture?*

'What's happening?' I asked Idehenre. The light-skinned six-footer had put on his dark glasses and getting set to leave too when he replied, 'You've not helped yourself.'

He called Lieutenant Hembal and ordered him to prepare a cell for me. I had become a coup suspect, and a prisoner.

At noon on March 5, 1995, Commander Omesa of the Nigerian Navy, who was the Chief Instructor of the junior division in Command and Staff College, Kaduna, was hungry. He went with his friend, Wing Commander K. Iyanayo, to a restaurant at the College's recreation centre. As they began eating, Iyanayo, who had just been posted to Port Harcourt, said, 'Have you heard that Bamgbose has been arrested?'

'What for?' Omesa asked.

'A coup they said, although I don't think he was involved in a plot of any kind.'

They talked about other things, not knowing that an Intelligence operative was sitting a short distance away, eavesdropping. The following day, Omesa was arrested and taken to one of the government houses, where he spent two weeks before he was transferred to Lagos in manacles with Lieutenant-Colonels Olu Bamgbose, Biodun Role, Femi Alaga, M.A. Igwe, D.A.D. Usman, Abibu Shuaibu and Major Muhammed.

When Iyanayo heard about the incident, he disappeared. Omesa suffered detention in Lagos like all the other officers arrested. The SIP could find nothing to hang on him. No one could help him, not even Commodore Mike Akhigbe, his close friend, who would later become Chief of General Staff in the regime of Abubakar.

Like Omesa, so many other officers and civilians also fell victim to the sadism and ineptitude of the DMI.

The human rights record under the regime of Buhari was dismal, and the institution responsible for it was the Nigerian Security Organisation (NSO) headed by Muhammadu Rafindadi. The power the NSO wielded under Rafindadi was so total that it turned Nigeria into an Orwellian State. Operating with the reach of an octopus, it recruited and handsomely rewarded university students, lecturers, labour activists and so many other freelance operatives who informed on their colleagues.

When Babangida assumed power on August 27, 1985, he saw the NSO as the powerhouse of the regime he had over- thrown. Appearing to dismantle it in order to gain popularity, he actually reorganised it and gave it a new name — the SSS. He made Brigadier Aliyu Mohammed Gusau, the first Director-General and put Rafindadi in jail. Babangida did all this to public acclaim. But the nation would soon realise that it had just escaped from a malevolent cobra only to jump into a hole full of scorpions. For a regime that many Nigerians would soon love to hate, a strong security base was needed. He also established the Directorate of Military Intelligence. By 1986, under its director, Akilu, the style of intelligence work shifted from detection to deterrence: to isolate and destroy, or eliminate all potential threats to the security of the self-styled military president. (The Directorate was now, in the main, for combat intelligence.)

Babangida indulged Akilu who received his own budgetary

illocation from the military as well as a lot of money from the presidency's unaudited security vote. Reports from the DMI converted the military president into a security-maniac. The more paranoid he became the more he thought he needed a safety valve in the DMI. One of the pet projects of Akilu was building the Security Group in 1986. This compact but ugly structure was located on 2 Park Lane, Apapa. This is where the DMI has its modern lock-up and its dungeon— unarguably the most dreaded underground prison in Nigeria. Its capacity for ruthless destruction did not become a source of genuine fear until Giwa was assassinated by a parcel bomb on October 19, 1986, just a few days after his interrogation by the DMI*. The directorate accused Giwa, among other things, of gunrunning and planning to stage a revolution, but many Nigerians still believe that he was murdered for investigating a drug story in which the family of the president was allegedly involved.

If Babangida forgot to ask Akilu and Lieutenant-Colonel A. K. Togun, then deputy director of the SSS, and other officers, any question about Giwa's death, he spat fire at the DMI after Major Gideon Orkar's coup attempt in which Babangida and his immediate family narrowly escaped death inside the presidential lodge at Dodan Barracks on April 22, 1990. His *aide-de-camp*, Colonel U.K. Bello, lost his life in that incident. For Babangida this was evidence of the incompetence of the DMI.

On his part, Abacha never liked Akilu as the director of the DMI because he was said to have written a damaging security report about him. When Abacha schemed his way to power on November 17, 1993, he quickly posted Akilu out of the National Intelligence Agency (NIA) in Bonny Camp, Lagos to the Army Resettlement, Recruitment and Rehabilitation Centre in Oshodi, Lagos. But then, before he reported at his new duty

---

* It was the week that Wole Soyinka won the Nobel Prize for Literature. Giwa had attended the party organised by Vera Ifudu to celebrate this coveted prize.

post, he was retired along with many of the officers who were close, or suspected to be close, to Babangida. He got to know of his retirement, on the network news of the Nigerian Television Authority (NTA).

The 1995 coup bogey reared its ugly head at a time when the DMI was in a state of fumbling transition: directors kept coming and going — Lieutenant-Colonel I. Karmashe, Togun, Brigadier-Generals M.C. Alli, Ahmed A.Abdullahi and Brigadier A.S. Muktar. (Muktar, a lawyer, who insisted there was no coup plot, was instantly removed). Before Colonel Sabo Muhammed was given the job, Lieutenant-Colonel Kola John Olu, the Commanding Officer of the Security Group unofficially acted as the director. Olu did not share Muktar's conviction that the coup was a rumour. He worked in concert with Abdullahi (who had become General Officer Commanding 1 Mechanised Division, Kaduna). Abdullahi was very much interested in using the coup to prove that Major-General Alwali Kazir, the new Chief of Army Staff, who had first insisted there was no coup plot, was incompetent. Abdullahi even opposed the appointment of Kazir as the Army Chief. Fueling the intrigue was the keen rivalry between the regular and the 'emergency' officers. (The 'emergency' officers were those ones who rose rapidly because of the exigency of the civil war.)

Such divisions caused leaks, and vital information found its way to the press. Yet Nigerian soldiers were forbidden from speaking except with the express permission of the Chief of Army Staff. Any soldier who flouted this regulation put his job on the line. It was clear to me that part of the initial objective of that interrogation was to fish out fifth columnists among the high-ranking officers in the military who were responsible for the torrent of official leaks.

The young officer took me to the soldier's ragged dressing room. The window panes were broken, the light bulb was dead, but there were three worn beds with two dirty, old single foam mattresses that smelled. I was locked up with no breakfast. No lunch. No dinner. Exhausted, I sat on one of the beds, amidst the buzz of mosquitoes, reviewing my encounter with the DMI's interrogators. *Why were they interested in telling me that they, too, were university graduates? What direction will the interrogation take tomorrow? Will it be unbearable?* I was supposed to hold a meeting with my mother that night to discuss my late father's property. *Would this arrest not compound her emotional problems?*

Less than two hours later, I heard the sentries open the main gate. A Maruti jeep drew up with three soldiers and a civilian. In the darkness of my cell I could see them without being seen. The civilian got out of the jeep and headed towards my cell. One of the soldiers opened the lock and pushed him inside. As soon as this stranger entered, he knelt down beside one of the two other beds. Not knowing that I was in the room, he began to pray:

'My Lord and my God, you know I'm your child. I don't belong to the devil. But I'm now in the den of evil men. If you don't deliver me, Satan will gloat over my defeat and ask: where is your God?…'

He went on and on, and I allowed him to demonstrate enough helplessness before I made some mock attempts at killing some mosquitoes. Surprised, he rounded off his prayer. Silence. Introductions. Realities. A stinking cell. The stranger was Ben Charles-Obi, the editor of *Weekend Classique,* who had been with the DMI since May 9, 1995.

He was arrested because of his lead story on Shuaibu, who was being used to frame some officers by alleging that they were coup plotters. The security was disturbed by the story because it not only discredited the SIP, it also, according to the Security Group, endangered Shuaibu's life. Olu and his officers in the Security Group tried to break Charles-Obi down with threats but he had refused to tell them his source. They told him that his story had caused a lot of trouble in the barracks, that many people were already calling Shuaibu a traitor and that his children had been ridiculed in school. Charles-Obi's reply was direct: 'I am not in a position to confirm what you are saying, but for me there are three things: Is the story true? Can it promote the practice of journalism? Can it help the cause of justice and equity?'

Expectedly, this angered them.

He had gone to the Security Group with his publisher, MEE Mofe-Damijo. He had not wanted to go but she persuaded him. 'She gave me the impression that she had sorted out the matter with them and that my going there was just a formality. But by 9:00 PM, she left, saying 'Ben, take it easy with them, co-operate with them.' When she had left, they said they would kill him if he did not tell them the source of the story, but if he co-operated they would release him. He knew they were lying.

Charles-Obi brought the news of the latest arrest of Chris Anyanwu, the publisher of *The Sunday Magazine* (*TSM*), on June 1, 1995. She had been arrested on March 15, 1995 after her magazine reported the early arrests of some officers. She was released on March 23. Charged by the Lagos State Commissioner of Police, she was accused of conspiring with Comfort Obi and Steve Ohakwe to 'publish false news items titled *Coup Update: Bloodbath Soon* and *Echoes of Coup Rock the Nation* with intent to cause fear and alarm to the public, thereby committing an offence punishable under section 517 of the criminal code'. *TSM*'s report of the coup had infuriated General Ike Nwachukwu, who had complained that he had not been arrested as the magazine had claimed. Anyanwu had gone to his house to apologise.

The latest arrest, from the account of the soldiers, could pass for abduction. On demanding to know who had ordered that she be arrested (or rather abducted) again, the arresting officer called the SIP to say Anyanwu was resisting arrest. Colonel Santuraki, who answered the telephone, then persuaded her to come in for questions, but as soon as she entered their car, the soldiers put her in handcuffs and drove off first to the venue of the panel in Ikoyi and then to the Security Group. She was subsequently moved to Maximum Security Prison, Kirikiri, as a coup suspect.

Not knowing where I was being held, my colleagues had declared my whereabouts unknown. I smuggled out a note to let them know where I was. How the press got to know that I was in the DMI became another matter for investigation. I wasn't contacted though, but I noticed that surveillance around me was intensified.

I asked if I could use their small library. Unexpectedly, permission was granted the following morning and I read newspapers legally plus a dog-eared copy of Arthur M. Schlesinger, Jr.'s *The Crisis of Confidence*. Schlesinger, Jr., an American historian, has a thoroughly captivating style. He temporarily made me forget my anguish. Writing about the dilemma of presidential power, he says:

> 'A president must, above all, be a man who acts not just because he himself is sure about the wisdom of a course of action but because he is responsive to the democratic process. It is not enough for policies to be sound…. He must understand the legitimacy of challenges to his own authority and wisdom. He must

cherish an inner skepticism about the anointment of
office and a constant awareness of what Whitman
called "the never-ending audacity of elected persons".
He must be especially skeptical about the unique value
of information that arrives through official channels
and about self-serving bureaucratic versions of anything. He must be sensitive to the diversity of concern and conviction in a nation; he must be sensitive
in advance to the verdict of history…'*

I remember quoting this passage from the book to
Majoyeogbe one afternoon in the course of our discussion. He
had been assigned the task of drawing me out informally since I
refused to talk or, as they say in the DMI, ' to sing formally'. He
would send old editions of *The Economist* to me in the morning and in the afternoon he would come to my cell to appeal to
me to name the source of our story. He played the *agent pro-
vocateur* very clumsily. He would say unprintable things about
Abacha and Diya. But each time I said *Oh no, I don't want to
talk about them*, he would back off.

However, the day General Abdulkarimu Adisa declared in
Ilorin that he knew those who planted the bombs that had exploded at the stadium where Mrs. Mariam Abacha was about
to launch the Kwara State's branch of the Family Support Programme (FSP), I said,

'Here you are Colonel. Just read this.' I pointed at the story
of the bomb explosion in the *Nigerian Tribune*. He browsed
through and looked at me,

'What do you think?', I asked.

'The man is very crude,' he answered.

'I agree. How can a General say this? If he knew those who
are responsible, he should be talking to the police. I suppose
the man doesn't have any clue as to who did what.'

* Arthur M. Schlesinger, Jr. *The Crisis of Confidence* (Boston: Houghton Mifflin, 1969).

I began to feel a little dizzy after this session. Suspecting malaria, I reported it to the Sergeant on duty. I was waiting for the doctor at noon the following day when the Regiment Sergeant-Major (RSM) of the DMI and a second Lieutenant burst into the cell and ordered me to sit up. The young officer then handed me two of the notes I had smuggled out the day before.

'Did you write these?'

I grimaced superciliously.

'Answer, now'

'Yes, I did'

And they left, *double quick.* An emergency meeting was called over the 'crime'. I became a victim of derision and hatred as I waited for the verdict of the people I had once again offended. *How did they intercept the notes? What would happen to my foot soldiers?* I wondered. As all the soldiers interrogated forcefully denied having anything to do with me (even the owner of the Bible in which the notes were found had denied the ownership of his own holy book!), the judges pleaded with me to identify the culprits. I told them I had no intention of doing so. They returned me to the cell and a few hours later, the RSM came to the cell and told me to pack.

'Where are you taking me?'

He did not reply. I asked him to let me return the two books I was reading to the library. I managed to whisper a message to a soldier who had become my friend: *they are taking me to an unknown destination. Please, tell my people.* Three soldiers joined the RSM to lead me out of the DMI on June 2, 1995.

Our destination was within a walking distance of the headquarters. The RSM banged the iron gate, and I was taken to the office of Lieutenant-Colonel Ayo Joshua, the Commanding

Officer of the Counter Intelligence Corps*. The place had a dreary air. It was dank and squalid. The soldiers looked hungry and Joshua, their Commander, enjoyed drinking one bottle too many.

News of my wrongdoing had spread. The unit took it upon itself to show that whatever little civility had previously been accorded me was over. I was marched to the punishment cell. When the soldier opened the fortified iron door, I heard a movement inside. *Was I going to be thrown amongst hoodlums? How would I survive in this place?* I imagined the agony that awaited me. After a thorough search of my pockets for any weapon, I was ordered inside. I stood in shock.

There I found a man lying almost naked on the damp floor. His eyes were bloodshot, his hair dishevelled, his skin scaly— he appeared not to have had a bath for days. He was chewing *alligator pepper* and *bitter kola*! The man was George Mbah, assistant editor of *TELL*. He had been arrested for a story published in the May 11, 1995 edition of *Dateline*, a sister publication. His story was about the sudden death of Major Sunday Oni.* The story implied that Oni's death had something to do with the alleged coup plot. It suggested that because Oni had not cooperated with his military interrogators, he was poisoned. (It seemed that he suddenly slumped behind the wheel of his car and died).

Information from a short interview that Mbah had with Lieutenant-Colonel Godwin Ugbo of the Defence Public Relations had been cited. Mbah was arrested for this reason on May 5, 1995. Four days later, he was taken to the Military Intelligence School, Apapa, where he was stripped of his shirt and his medi-

---

* Because the DMI had no troops of its own, this unit was created to take charge of its increasingly combatant duties which consisted mainly of arrests and the liquidation of enemies.

* Commander, Army Intelligence Corps attached to the 33 Field Artillery Brigade, Bauchi.

cation*. He said he was forced to urinate and defecate on the floor of his cell and was kept in this cell without the option of a bath for a month. The soldiers wanted the source of his story and the addresses of his editorial directors.

Majoyeogbe had been aggrieved by the story in *Dateline*.

'How could they have imputed that we poisoned our colleague who died of a heart attack?' he asked. 'We all went to his burial and paid him our last respects. It's only the police people who always kill each other'.

So, this is the much-talked about hellhole. Has my life come to this: a cell fetid with stench? I thought as I surveyed the eight-by-four cell. No electricity, no windows— just a small opening to let in some air. The walls were splashed with the blood of former occupants. Shortly after they had locked me up, they brought Charles-Obi. Shell-shocked, we looked like prisoners of war. I slept as did the others, molested by mosquitoes.

The iron door of the cell was left ajar. I looked around. My cellmates had left. *Why have they left me* alone *here?* I wondered. *And where had all the sentries gone?* As an eerie atmosphere descended on the cell, I looked at the clear sky and envied the stars their freedom. Scared, I left the cell, running. I was now in a jungle littered with bones of human beings and animals. I tried to escape from it, only to discover that three pythons were chasing me. As I ran, I stumbled on the butchered remains of more people. Depleted, I sat for a while on the crest of a hill. I was free, and I knew I would get home in a day or two. I woke up panting. My freedom was a bad dream. I was confused. Depressed, I smuggled this short note to my wife on June 23, 1995:

---

* Medication was for a head injury in a car accident.

My dear Bunmi,

How are you, Mayowa, my mom, our neighbours and all the members of our extended families? I would have written you again since I was brought to DMI, but I changed my mind because I did not want to expose you to any danger.

I've written to inform my colleagues that the government of Abacha has made up its mind to deal with us ruthlessly. How will this end? I do not know. But I know that I'll come home, one day, with my head unbowed.

Pls, Bunmi,while I'm gone, be a confident manager of our home. Don't let anybody see you as an object of pity. I've not committed any crime. It is those who are treating me shabbily who should be treated with absolute contempt because they are the criminals.

I won't break down. I pray that God will see us through this difficult time. Give my regards to everyone.

With much love.
Kunle.

We were allowed to go out once a day, in the evening, under an armed guard, to have a bath. We were told to urinate into bottles they provided and pour our urine outside through the small opening. Of course, after two weeks, the smell of urine was overpowering. We had to wait till evening to use the toilet. To grind our spirits down further, we each received only twenty naira a day for food. This we passed on to the soldiers on duty to help us buy junk food. In no time, we began to lose weight but we managed to keep sane.

I did not want to fall ill in that life-threatening environment, but I was aware that determination alone was an inadequate prophylactic. Night after night, lying there, unable to sleep, I knew it was just a question of time before I broke down. It had become hard to ward off malaria fever.

As I lay ill with a raging fever, I watched soldiers on night duty sleep with prostitutes; I watched an officer steal new car tyres seized from a dealer at the border; I saw some civilians beaten to pulp and still made to frog-jump over the gutters; and observed the soldiers stay for two nights, fully armed, ready for the customary protests about June 12*. When I learnt that Chief Michael Adekunle Ajasin, the chosen political leader of the Yoruba, and some members of *Afenifere** were arrested and detained for holding a political meeting in Owo, I knew the clampdown on politicians likely to organise rallies against Abacha on June 12 had begun. I still retained a comforting illusion, even when the coup trial commenced on June 5, 1995, that we would not be tried as well. I was wrong.

In the morning of July 7, 1995, as I tried to rise, the cell whirled around me. I wanted to shout for help but my voice was too weak. I threw up blood. My fellow inmates banged the door calling for help.

'Oh, I'm in trouble!' was the last sentence I uttered before I collapsed.

This was the day in 1993 when Chief M.K.O. Abiola, going by the accounts of various election monitoring groups, which included foreign observers, won a presidential election. The first Nigerian to win large votes across religious and ethnic barriers. But Babangida cancelled the results.

The pan-Yoruba political, social and cultural association.

FOUR

~~~~

Charged with New Energy

I lay still as the white Maruti jeep took me to the Military Hospital, Ikoyi. I felt nauseous. In my state of semi-consciousness, I kept muttering to myself: *will I ever return from this perilous trip*? We pulled up at the hospital known simply as Creek. Like a log of wood, I was offloaded and taken to the Emergency Ward where Dr. Lawson put me on intravenous fluids.

I stayed all night in the Emergency Ward with Lieutenant-Colonel Okiki, the former Chairman of the Rivers State Transport Corporation, who was brought in from a cell at the intercentre* amidst heavy security by infantry soldiers. He was branded a coup-suspect.*

Just before Okiki was arrested in connection with the phantom coup, he had a problem with the Military Administrator of Rivers State, Lieutenant-Colonel Dauda Komo. He had written to the Head of State, asking him to look into the disburse-

---

* Interrogation Centre; the SSS detention camp which shared a boundary with a cemetry.

* Okiki led the operation that quelled the Maitatsine religious riots in Jimeta, Yola.

ment of a large sum of money, which he was sure the Administrator had embezzled. In the same letter, he accused Komo of smuggling petroleum products on the high seas. Unfortunately, the note was intercepted and passed on to the accused, who was enraged and ordered that Okiki be locked up in the soldiers' guardroom where the writer and environmental activist, Saro-Wiwa, was being held.

Recalling his meeting with Saro-Wiwa, Okiki said: 'He is a very articulate man fighting for a just cause. I am Ijaw from Rivers State and aware of the problems involved. What is happening in Ogoni is sad. I have said many times that detaining the true representatives of the Ogoni will not solve the problems. Ken was very kind to me throughout our stay together. He was generous too. A very good fighter, he cheered me up. When I was about to be taken away, he offered very useful advice: 'Look, my friend', he whispered to me, 'if the authority wants to kill you struggle for your life; don't just give in.*

When Okiki appeared before the SIP in chains, he was surprised to hear it was because of an alleged coup. He was accused of setting up a special account from the money made in the Rivers State Transport Corporation to bankroll a resistance movement set up by Major Akinloye Akinyemi, a man he had never met. In spite of all the torture he was subjected to, Akinyemi also told the SIP that he had written down Okiki's name without his knowledge. In the end, Okiki was not convicted but given a stern warning to stay away from the press.

Within a week in the hospital I regained my appetite. Food was provided with the help of the hospital's matron, Lieutenant-Colonel (Mrs.) C. O. Okunola. With the warmth and assurances of the nurses, and the solicitude of the doctors,

---

* Saro-Wiwa was later hanged along with eight of his Ogoni kinsmen by the regime of Abacha.

I began to feel comfortable and relaxed. But my face and feet were still swollen, I had to be formally admitted, therefore, to the hospital by the Commanding Officer, Lieutenant-Colonel (Dr.) Femi Awofeso. In the CO's office, I saw a reflection in the mirror. It was of a body shrivelled. It alarmed me. That ghost of myself was still in his bloodstained, sweat-soaked *adire** shirt and trousers; his uncut hair was rough and his beard was overgrown. No: that was not even my ghost. It was the casualty of a senseless civil strife long forgotten in a desert.

As I lay on the bed, my worried mind travelled to the various homes of my loved ones. I contemplated the fate of Nigeria in the hands of Abacha, the success-starved man. I recalled that Ofeimun, had speculated in an essay he wrote for *TheNEWS* in 1994 titled *Abacha as Pinochet* that the dark-goggled general would try to ape and match the Chilean model of military dictatorship. Ofeimun argued that there was a chemistry of personalities and events at work in Nigeria at that moment which made it critical to recall the Chilean mayhem as both a warning and a possibility. He cautioned that it was wrong to say that what happened in Chile could not happen in Nigeria. He pointed out that there were telltale signs that Abacha would rule by dictatorial fiat. His reading was that a government which claimed to have come for National Reconciliation, but had locked up the acclaimed winner of the presidential election, was deadly serious about its own ambition.

When Ofeimun submitted that piece for publication, I had told him that he was giving undue credit to the intelligence of Abacha by comparing him to Pinochet. But Ofeimun's speculation began to have a force of certainty in those gory moments.

I thought of detention without trial, imprisonment of innocent people, torture centres, the muzzling of the press, the persecu-

---

* Tie and dye

tion of labour, student leaders, intellectuals and politicians of the left. I thought of so many Chilean exiles and the criminalised ones who just disappeared.

Is Abacha our own punishment for general indolence and tacit support of tyranny? Is this the resurgence of evil on our political terrain? How can we be saved from the fangs of our own dark- goggled dictator?

The loud, hollow sounds of soldiers' boots on the concrete relieved me of the burden of introspection. The emissaries of agony had come from the Security Group, holding fake compassion in one hand and handcuffs in another. They put me in chains. The officer in charge detailed two armed soldiers to guard me in the cubicle, an unnecessary precaution in a military hospital with its armed soldiers. The comfort I was beginning to enjoy now tasted like sand in my mouth.

They brought the evening meal. For a long time, I did not touch the food. I just could not bring myself to do so. One of the soldiers pleaded with me,

'Make you chop, now'

No reply.

'You dey vex?'

I looked at him and said, 'It's not possible for me to eat, handcuffed'.

'Why you no talk since, now? I get the key here. We suppose to open you when you wan chop and lock you when you finis'.

I looked carefully at the handcuffs on my wrists. They were new. Made in Germany. How portable they seemed. I told the soldier not to bother.

'I am not hungry. You can have my food'.

I slipped under the blanket and lay curled up on the bed, turning down every appeal not to skip my meal. Night gently fell on the heels of this troublesome evening. By 10:00 PM , I had already drifted into sleep when the soldier with the key woke me up and said, *'Sorry o! We suppose to chain you to this bed when you wan sleep.'*

'How can you...?' I wanted to protest. He quickly unlocked the handcuff, put my right hand in one of the holes and hooked the other to the topmost rail of the strong iron bed. Job finished, he went to sleep soundly, leaving me there to stare at the ceiling.

As sleep fled, I suffered a wild beating in my head. It was midnight. I wanted to know how far my health had deteriorated, so I called the nurse on duty who in turn called the doctor. I did not know that I had become significantly repellent until the tall, attractive, dainty and young female doctor wearing a fashionable *boubou* flinched at the sight of me. She stood at a respectful distance while attending to me. I made some effort to sit up but could not. It occurred to me that I should assure the woman that I was not mad. But the little effort I made was further confirmation of her suspicions. She had fished out a new thermometer from her handbag. I admired it.

'Isn't that cute?' I said.

She ignored me, but gave me a look that said, *And so what*? I was not mollified.

I looked back at her calmly and said, 'It's a shame, isn't it, that about five years to the twenty-first century we're not thinking of making a simple thing like that instrument. It's a shame, a damn shame'.

It was a trite observation. But it proved something: that we still fought for the most ordinary banalities in my country. Things that were taken for granted in other places we spent the most productive part of our lives dreaming to acquire.

The thermometer fascinated me, but that was not all. The

woman was also the object of my fascination. Surrounded by armed soldiers, I wanted a decent person like her to relate to me, not as a coup suspect, but as a human being. But she was afraid.

The matron came to see me first thing in the morning, having read the report that I had embarked on hunger strike. I didn't have to explain why, for she too could see the way I was bound to the bed. She stared angrily at the soldiers as she paced the floor of the cubicle.

'Look here, what do you think you're doing? Where do you think you are? This is not Security Group, you hear. This is not DMI. This is Creek. You have brought this man here for treatment. Let's do our job, you hear. Now loose him. LOOSE HIM. Let him take his bath, his breakfast and his drugs. You! Yes, you. Take him to the bathroom.' Her tone was uncompromising.

The order of Olu that I be chained for twenty-four hours was therefore amended to: handcuffs between 10:00 PM and 10:00 AM. I was worried about my deteriorating health. The three doctors in charge of my case—Drs. Lawson, Fisher and Nwachukwu recommended that I should have a barium meal test done, and the Security Group was informed that it should provide money for the somewhat expensive test. The Commanding Officer of the Security Group ignored the request. Instead, he sent his RSM to tell me to lie to the doctors that I was well. The RSM presented that to me in a smooth way, saying that if I stayed too long in that hospital I might contact a communicable disease. When he finished, I responded: 'Thank you, RSM! I don't want to continue staying here. The problem is that these doctors won't let me go without the test. They are the ones insisting I must have the test. Please, tell your CO to sort things out with the man in charge of this place so that I can get out of this *terrible* place in a short while.'

He put his swagger stick under his armpit and we shook hands. He was happy that I was polite. Stiff in his uniform, Adjarho walked away. The attempt to lure me out of the hospital had failed.

The hospital, completed in 1976, was built to give first class treatment to all ailing military officers and their relations. But the outward purity of it was a façade covering the decay inside which held so much attraction for many rats, roaches and mosquitoes. Whenever the wind wafted through my cubicle, the pungent odour of faeces and urine in the old, tired and stained lavatories, the crusts, the mossy floors and peelings on the walls could put your bowels on hold.

While I was there, the Ministry of Defence had not paid the civilian staff for two months. The fortunes of the hospital dwindled as rapidly as the country itself. Particularly noticeable was the food the hospital served its patients: small pap with sugar in the morning and two slices of yam with stew in the evening. Albeit, it was still better than the niggardly dish prepared at the Security Group and served to all the coup suspects: a wrap of solid *Eba* with o*kro* soup every afternoon.

My long stay in Creek (July 7 – September 8, 1995) was both harsh and rewarding. It was there that I learned of our trial and imprisonment long before they happened. It was there that I got to know that Nigeria had lost more than 5,000 soldiers and officers in the so-called peacekeeping operation in Liberia. And it was from this hospital that I appeared twice (July 17 and 18, 1995) before the Mujakperuo SIP and twice (July 28 and

29, 1995) before the SMT. As my mind struggled to find an anchor in this unbearably suffocating place, I was anxious about when I would be allowed to draw a free breath again.

One of the officers keeping peace in Liberia, Lieutenant-Colonel L. Aprezi, was wheeled to my cubicle late August, after a sinusitis operation.

'What you people don't realise is that Nigeria cannot afford to have a disintegrated continent. We cannot share the limited resources we have now with refugees who would invade this country if Liberia packs up. It is better to prevent a holocaust in Liberia in order to save Nigeria. My problem with you guys in the media is that you just sit at home criticising those of us in the battle field, doing our legitimate job. Leave your desks. Come to the warfront. That's where the action is.'

He wiped the viscous flow of blood in his nostrils, adjusted his pillow and rested his head on it, waiting for me to reply.

'You and I know that it's not fair to accuse the Nigerian media that has lost two journalists in that savagery of sitting at home to criticise.'

When the revolt in Liberia resulted to genocide in 1990, Krees Imodibie of *The Guardian* and Tayo Awotunsin of *Daily Champion*, who had gone to Liberia to cover the beginning of that internecine were killed. The third journalist, Frank Igwebueze, a colleague of mine in *African Concord*, was evacuated from the scene of the carnage by the American Embassy. Despite the murder of Imodibie, another journalist from *The Guardian*, Kayode Komolafe, was sent to cover Liberia. I told him that there were soldiers and officers who were trading in arms and ammunition in Liberia. There were businessmen, too, in government who were profiteering from the war in Liberia. Those ones would not want the war to end.

Aprezi smiled a little and demanded, 'Evidence, my brother. Give me evidence. Who and who are the people trading in Liberia? Tell me. Who are these people?'

The soldiers had now gathered in our cubicle to listen to our conversation.

'There is no point mentioning names. You know them.'

Aprezi's wife and his two children, a boy and a girl, brought some get-well cards from home, but he concentrated his attention on his pretty wife. Strong feelings suddenly stirred in my heart for my wife: *how was she coping with the problem of my detention?* I was very afraid that she could lose the pregnancy. I wanted to see her urgently if only to cushion her pain a little. But the State prevented that.

My mind drifted to the casualties of the Liberian crisis, who had been used and discarded by the Nigerian military. Many of those wounded soldiers were moved from the Military Hospital, Yaba, in 1993 to the Murtala Muhammed International Airport from where, with all fanfare, they were flown to Cairo for what was going to be specialist treatment. But as it turned out, Hassabo International Hospital in Cairo rejected the soldiers on the ground that they were not fresh cases. From then on, soldiers who had lost their limbs, or had gone blind, began to lose hope as well.

August 26, 1995. Our cubicle was unusually quiet. Aprezi concentrated on a novel. Denied the right to read any other printed matter besides *The Holy Bible* and *The Holy Quran,* I opened to the book of *Lamentations*, which, for me, has always been a fascinating literary text. Suddenly, Aprezi broke the silence,

'Look, my friend. Things are not so easy for our rulers. It's a complex country. We should pity them rather than blame them.

There are so many interests competing for attention and how many of them can you satisfy? It's difficult, my brother. Sometimes a government may decide that it is going in one direction only to find itself facing another direction. You can only appreciate that detour if you have patience and understanding.'

'If a government goes in a wrong direction that means it has lost it. Why should we waste time trying to understand such a government? Let it quit instead of wasting our precious time.' I answered.

I now had his full attention: 'This incessant attack on every military administration in this country is very unhealthy. You people said Buhari was tyrannical and he was overthrown. You said Babangida was a liar and a murderer, and you forced him to step aside. Now, you say that Abacha is wicked, that he is a thief. What do you want? What do you want? Tell me?'

I said flatly, 'We'd love for the armed forces to go back to their barracks. They've outlived their usefulness. We have examined you very carefully and we've found that you are bereft of leadership qualities. Consider Buhari rough-shod rule. Under Babangida, corruption almost became a state policy. I am in chains now because somebody in Aso Rock is a lunatic.'

I know the value of silence at grim moments like this. I was not naïve as not to know that some of the officers I discussed with were actually spies. I had decided to surrender all dread to all those who were afraid of truth and who, with utmost zest, were preparing to kill us. I knew that the military profession in Nigeria had lost its shine. And it would require a sense of responsibility to the nation on the part of any leader to make the military a true national fighting force.

Politicised and tribalised, the military was a wrecked institution in 1995. Officers who got local and foreign appointments did not get them on merit. Performance in Command and Staff College, which ought to serve as a means of evaluation, was no longer considered. Officers lobbied strenuously for foreign appointments.

There existed in the military a class of prosperous officers who were lording it over the indigent ones, mostly bright officers from the southern part of Nigeria. The brilliant but poor officers did not complain loudly; they might tell you—*Oh, no hard feelings: it's the fault of the system,* but their children did complain. Their wives, some of whom I met in the hospital, complained endlessly.

Consider this example: In December 1994, two directing staff at the Command and Staff College arrived at the departure lobby of the Kaduna Airport. Being holiday time, they also met some pupils of the Nigerian Military School (NMS) milling around in their military khaki attire looking spiffy. As the boys sighted the two officers, they gave them an impressive salute. One of the officers started talking to one of the boys about his career choice in the military. The 17-year-old boy was in senior secondary class two. He told the officer, 'I am not interested in the military. I'm not interested in a job where you can only make it through who you know.' The jolted officer turned to his colleague, and said, 'See what a small boy knows about us.'

Under the control of a northern military clique, the military had three principal ways of eliminating southern officers, or vocal officers. They might try luring them with money. If they were not careful with that money, they would be accused of embezzlement and then shown the door. They might frustrate them deliberately to gauge their temperament. For instance, their promotion might be delayed for no reason. If they complained, they would be labelled disgruntled elements and kicked out. Such officers were also framed.

By 1995, the equipment that the military had was obsolete. Many of the logistics vehicles were grounded. In spite of the huge amount of money voted for the Ministry of Defence, which Abacha ran for eight years, soldiers lived in slums. There was the numerical problem as well. The Army had close to 80,000 staff, the Navy about 12,000 and the Air Force approximately 11,000. It was amazing that many of the bright officers I spoke with were not sure of their numerical strength. What was clear, however, was that the Nigerian armed forces need to be modernised.

It also struck me that the civil society always fails to crush the inordinate ambition of the politicians in uniform because of its huge ignorance of the military. Most of the time, defence reports are based mainly on lies dished out by some military officers whose job has been turned, over the years, into covering up the rot in the system. This attitude prevents the public from sniffing the stench of dictatorship before it wafts to the center-stage of the nation's political life.

The terror of the SIP came July 15, 1995 in the form of Captain Bashir Mormoni.

If there was any doubt as to whether I was going to be tried or not, the form he gave me to fill out put it to rest.

'In the last two years, which places did you visit and for what purpose?'; 'Which policies of the current regime do you prefer?'; 'What do you think about the regimentation in the army?'; 'How many cars do you have and how did you acquire them?'; 'What's your foreign account number?'; 'What's your passport number?'; 'Which schools did you attend?'; 'Your names, state, religion, height, weight, age and nationality?'; 'What is your Army/Navy/Airforce number?'; 'What is your corps?'; 'What is your rank?' etc., etc.

I knew better than to fill out the form without my lawyer's consent. But given the history of contempt for civilised procedures by successive military regimes in Nigeria, I thought that if I brought in my lawyer, Falana, he might also end up in detention. I also knew I could be manhandled or beaten up if I did not fill out the form. Did a military officer not hurt Olorunyomi's fingers in Bonny Camp because he refused to write a statement in 1994? More importantly, I knew it would not be in my interest to show at that point that I would not cooperate with the SIP, knowing that they could slate me for physical torture. I therefore decided to fill out the form with absolute caution. Since it was a questionnaire basically designed for soldiers, I said, 'Officer, this form is not meant for civilians'.

Mormoni scanned through the form and said, 'Sure. Just fill out the areas that concern you', which I did.

The following Monday, the military police attached to the SIP came to the Military Hospital and pulled me out of bed. Outraged and amazed, the Commanding Officer of the hospital, Awofeso, wrote to the panel, complaining of the inappropriateness of that action.

In the military truck parked in front of the hospital, I met Mbah bound in chains, looking ruffled but still feisty. As soon as he saw me, he raised his chained hands in salute. I acknowledged with a chuckle. As the truck moved into top gear, belching, cutting through the glitter of Awolowo Road, Ikoyi, I asked him how much shock he was ready to absorb. Agitated, he replied, 'Are they planning to kill us?' Based on the information I had received, I told him that Abacha had decided to jail us. What we were about to witness, then, both at the SIP and the SMT, was an enactment of a written text.

We arrived at our destination at 8:35 AM, but the interrogation did not start until 2:05 PM, giving me ample time to size up the territory of the uniformed sadists. The observatory was the unplastered waiting room. I saw many of the newly-minted handcuffs dumped on an iron-bed; many cartons of natural spring water; jubilant cooks passing plates of sumptuous food. *Were they celebrating a mini festival of plenitude? Or, as they shared the booty of Abacha, were they celebrating the carnival of imminent deaths?* There was no doubt that they were given plenty of money for this exercise.

As I sat in that room, I also heard spasmodic groans of people in pain. *Oh, who were those people groaning? Who were those men whose anguish freely joined our own pains?* *

While we waited, the soldiers on duty regaled us with salacious story of the exploits of Nigerian soldiers on the United Nations peace keeping mission in Somalia. It was painful to hear them chatting flippantly about the profound tragedy of a ruptured, bleeding continent. They raved about the Somali women who offered themselves cheap for American dollars.

---

* They were Colonels Gabriel Ajayi and R.S.B. Bello-Fadile. They had released details of their defense notes to the press and human rights groups.

FIVE

~~~~~

Facing the
Inquisitors

The Mujakperuo SIP in Ikoyi sat in secret. No one who appeared before it had access to counsel and then voluntary statements were twisted to make the incredible look true. It used torture and coercion to collect its evidence. The guilty passed harsh judgement on the innocent. Many members of the panel took pleasure in observing their chained compatriots weep before them.

The SIP was divided into three units: Interrogation, Investigation and Legal. If you appeared before any of the teams and were found culpable, you would then be sent to the Investigation unit, which would send you to the SMT with a charge prepared by the Legal unit.

It was the prerogative of each unit to apply whatever mode of interrogation it chose. This was why people alleged to have committed identical crimes were subjected to different forms of torture. The grand deception style seemed to be the preferred

tactic of the panel. Lieutenant-Colonel Frank Omenka and Assistant Commissioner of Police (ACP), Hassan Zakari Biu,
would prepare a statement, credit it to an alleged offender and
ask him to accept it. If he refused, they would blindfold him,
hang him upside down like a chicken ready for roasting.

In this position, they would once again ask the 'offender' to
make an admission of guilt. Forced statements were used to
implicate others. Lieutenant-Colonel Adesunloye was con-
fronted with a statement purportedly made by his room-mate*,
Colonel Oloruntoba, stating that he had told Adesunloye about
the coup plot. Adesunloye pleaded for Oloruntoba to repeat
the statement in his presence, but nothing was done. Eventually, Adesunloye was allowed home. Colonel Lawan Gwadabe
and many other officers were not so lucky: they were physically tortured.

Gwadabe had his legs tied together like a cow ready for
slaughter. Then ropes were drawn up suspending him upside
down; then minutes later, the ropes were further drawn up and
he was spread on a rack even while his legs were tied and his
hands cuffed to his back. A long pole was inserted between his
arms. Suspended thus, Biu asked him whether he was ready to
talk. Gwadabe stated that he knew nothing about a plot to overthrow the Abacha government. By the time they returned him
to the SIP, he was almost paralysed. Colonels G.A Ajayi, R.S.B.
Bello-Fadile, Olusegun Oloruntoba, Lieutenant-Colonel M.A.
Ajayi and Major Akinyemi were all tortured in the same manner.

After his first round on the torture machine, Akinyemi told
his torturers that he had nothing to say. The second round rendered him unconscious. For several minutes they thought he
was dead until one of them discovered that he was sweating,

---

* in Command and Staff College, Jaji.

so he said angrily, '*dead bodi no dey sweat now*!' Akinyemi was further hooked to the machine. This third round almost paralysed him.

I heard the continuing moans of the embattled officers. I was afraid of what could happen to me here. *If they hung me up and applied the electric prod, would I still have the courage to say no to their request for the source of our story? If military officers had surrendered in the torture chambers, would a civilian like me be able to withstand the pain*? I prayed that God would give me the courage and wisdom to make these opportunists in uniform look stupid.

My interrogators were four men in mufti: Lieutenant-Colonel Santuraki, the notorious Biu, Frank Omenka and Commander G. Akpollo. As I sank into the lone empty chair before them, Omenka, officer from the DMI who had his tobacco, big pipe and a copy of the May 29 edition of *TheNEWS* on his table, broke the silence:

'We understand that you are an ex-student of the University of Ife. What's your impression of that institution?'

I glanced at my handcuffs, which denied me the freedom to gesticulate.

'A brilliant idea, that University. A seedbed of a radical tradition in this country'

'How was it like being a Union executive?'

'I was never in the Students Union Government.'

'Where were you?'

'I was in the press.'

'But the rest of your colleagues were in the SUG?'

'No.'

'None of them contested for any post?'

'None. But they were like kingmakers.'

He opened the file on his table, checked through a document, 'now your company, Independent Communications Network Limited, is not a registered outfit.'

'Do you have any evidence to prove that?'

A pause. No evidence. Omenka picked up his pipe. He struck a match that didn't light. He tried again this time successfully. He then puffed arrogantly.

'Well, the organisation is a registered concern,' I said.

'Who is the publisher of *TheNEWS*?', Biu cut in.

'The publisher of *TheNEWS* is the Independent Communications Networks Limited'

Babel of voices expressed incredulity.

'Don't hide anything from us in your own best interest. Are you telling us that this magazine has no sponsor, that there is nobody financing it?' queried Omenka.

'We have directors, but no single one of them is the publisher.'

'Who are your directors?'

I gave them fake names, a gamble because if they had adequate information from the Corporate Affairs Commission they would have called me a liar and that would have diminished my confident pose as 'a witness of truth.' But they did not have the information.

'When did you establish the organisation?'

'That's a matter already in the public domain. Isn't it?'

'When?', Omenka shouted.

'1993.'

'Where did you get the money to start?' Biu asked.

'From some of our friends.'

'Who are these friends?'

Again, I did not hesitate to give them fake names.

Then suddenly, in a burst of madness, as if he was a marionette being controlled by a puppeteer, Omenka, stood up.

Pipe in mouth, he came for me and tigthened the handcuffs. Returning to his seat, he said:

'We are 50:50. The next stage is very delicate. If you don't tell us the truth, you will die. You will face a firing squad. Maybe when you get to heaven or hell, God will still punish you for this rubbish you've published. We shall use this story to show you that you people are clowns. We shall use you to teach other stupid liars a good lesson. That's the only way to stop all this nonsense.'

I thought the man was a lunatic.

Omenka opened his file and read out the list of the detained suspects from a magazine.

'Do you know that one of the officers included here died in 1992 in the Charlie130 NAF Hercules aircrash in Lagos? Do you know that? You people are a bunch of bastards. You are clowns. The ghost of this man, I am very sure, will not let you rest in peace in your own grave.'

Omenka was obviously mixing things up. The item was not in our story. *Where did he* get *the name*? I knew that what he glibly cited was not in The*NEWS*. I went on the attack:

'But this error is nothing when compared to the blunder the military made during the burial of the victims of that tragedy. How come that a southern officer who had gone to Abuja to witness the burial found his name on one of the cenotaphs? What would you call that morbid incident? A deliberate error? Grim, sad humour?'

What then happened was an anticlimax. The four *wise* men decided I should go to another room to write a statement based on the interrogation. I summarised the proceedings but wrote a fairly lengthy piece on the tyrannical tone of the encounter. I accused the panel of engaging in unnecessary persecution. Even if we had committed any error, I suggested, the interrogators should have handled the matter more effectively in a different way. What offence had we committed to deserve all the agony I had been subjected to? I concluded by asking them to search their consciences.

It was over by nightfall. I was returned to the hospital, naively thinking that I had finished with those sadists and courtiers, those lap dogs of stolen power.

B ut very early the following morning the military police returned. Since I was not expecting them, they had to wait for me to brush my teeth, take a quick shower and get dressed. This time they sought permission from the Commanding Officer of the hospital. After another long wait, I was led to one of the rooms upstairs where the Investigation unit sat with all its recording facilities. They were in military attire, except for one frail officer in *agbada*. As I sat down, Mujakperuo, who had read the statement I wrote the previous night, began,

'This investigation panel wants to assure you that it does everything with the fear of God. Our consciences are *clear*. You will be given a fair trial. Just answer our questions as simply as they are put to you. First, what is the role of an editor in *TheNEWS*?'

'He or she is the civilian equivalent of a Commanding Officer in the army. He calls the shots.'

'In other words, he is liable for any problem that arises from his magazine?'

'Yes.'

'Where did you get your material for this particular edition of your magazine.' Mujakperuo pointed at the controversial copy.

'I don't know.'

'You don't know, or you don't want to tell us?'

'I just don't know.'

'And you said the editor is a Commanding Officer?'

'I said he is like a Commanding Officer.'

'You must be an irresponsible Commanding Officer. You are not prepared to tell us the truth. But we shall soon find out when all the writers of this story are brought here.'

I was then asked to leave. As I stepped into the corridor, I was called back by Lieutenant-Colonel Hassan.

'Sit down. Sit down there.'

The mood of the house was a fighting one as Mujakperuo showed me one of the intercepted stories I had tried to smuggle out of the DMI.

'Did you write this?'

'Yes, I did.'

'Where did you write it?'

' In the DMI.'

'You were under detention then. Were you not?'

'Yes.'

'And you think that was the place to write this kind of rubbish?'

I didn't answer.

'Did you speak with anybody to confirm the story?'

'Nobody.'

'Junk Journalism. You write a story and publish it without confirming it?'

I did not reply.

The story was about the arrest of Lieutenant-Colonel Alaga and the maltreatment of the detainees in the DMI. That story was intended for *A.M NEWS*.

Colonel Yusuf, who sported a capped gold tooth and who had not said a word since the interrogation started, asked with a sneer, 'Are you a Nigerian?'

It was another silly question that did not deserve an answer.

Mujakperuo now holding the edition of *TEMPO,* which carried the defence of Bello-Fadile, asked, 'Do you also publish this?'

'Yes, *TEMPO* is one of our publications.'

'Get out. Take him away! Take him away!'

With that growl like that of a mad dog, I knew the panel was satisfied, that it had gotten enough evidence to prosecute me.

When they took me back to the hospital, I critiqued my performance and considered the gains and losses. I repeated in my mind this survival mantra: *They want to show me that I'm nothing. But I will stand up to them gracefully. They want me to believe that this is the end. But I will not give in to despair. I will survive. I WILL survive the tyrant.* I then went to the toilet to write a note to my colleagues, warning them that all those who reported the controversial cover story should take cover or run. Once again, they became a group of furtive exiles in their own land as they went underground.

SIX

~~~~

Dark Hours
Prolonged

The air was heavy as the *Black Maria was* taking the alleged coup suspects to the SMT on July 13, 1995. Chief Meredith Adisa Akinloye was one of them. Bamgbose greeted Chief Akinloye in Yoruba and asked, 'Sir, what allegation have they levelled against you?' Akinloye replied, 'They said I conspired to plan a *coup d'etat* with one Mr. Bello!'

He did not know that the man sitting next to him was Bello-Fadile. Also unknown to him, the tribunal had decided to set him free that day along with Mrs Titilayo Ajanaku, Yinka Johnson, Abbas Muazu, Akin Ogunpola and Folorunsho Sangoleye. That morning Lieutenant-Colonels Sambo Dasuki, Gabriel Anthony Nyiam, Benson Ikpe, Anthony Awoluyi and Great Ogboru were declared wanted.

I s this their court?'
Dr. Tokunbo Sofola* asked. She was brought in hand-cuffs to the SMT on July 28, 1995. Shell-shocked in her *adire* boubou, she could not help sobbing. Her question was not directed at any of us, but I recall saying, 'yes'. She started sobbing again. It was time for my first appearance. Bound in chains and handcuffs, I was led to the room with COURT IN PROGRESS written on the door.

Sitting to the right was the prosecution team led by Colonel Saibu. On the left were defense lawyers. The recording team was in front of them. On the right were the prosecution lawyers. In front of them was the dock with a military police. To complete the T-structure were members of the tribunal in two rows behind a table with two microphones on it. In the centre of all this was a wooden bench on which I, the accused, was positioned.

I barely managed to look composed. I kept my nerves steady as I looked at the tribunal members, the purveyors of the diverting macabre drama I was about to watch. *No question about it*, I said to myself, *this is a collection of self-deluded errand boys, this gang of Abacha's executioners. Some of them were mere criminals, yet they were parading themselves as the guardians of truth.* These people, I guessed, did not believe in what they were doing. It was merely a show of shameless bootlicking and complete absence of self-worth. For it was only a consciously corrupt or morally blind person that would collaborate with the evil schemes of Abacha. I felt like throwing a weapon, any weapon, at them. *Where, where is Aziza among them?* I asked myself.

Just then the clerk of the court performed his allotted role. He banged the table thrice and shouted: COU-OU-OU-R-T !

---

* Daughter of Chief Kehinde Sofola, a Senior Advocate of Nigeria.

We all stood up. The door of the inner chambers was flung open and a scarecrow of a judge entered with flourish. He took a slight bow. 'Be seated', he said. Like a muezzin getting set to make a call to Muslim salat, he tested the microphone. He then cast a sly, surreptitious glance at Lieutenant-Colonel Nathaniel Madza, the Judge-Advocate. He looked beyond him to his right and then to his left. Satisfied, he tested the microphone again and, finally, he nodded slightly to the cameramen to start filming the proceedings. I experienced a strange mixture of fascination and contempt. When the self-vaunting judge squinted at me, I remembered immediately a popular professional jester based in Lagos, whom I thought this character must be parodying. *What kind of shallow, comic show is this? Why is this mimic wasting our time?*

Aziza began to read the convening order signed by the Chief of Defence Staff, Abubakar: 'The tribunal was set up under section 40 subsection 1 and 2 of the Criminal Code and Treason and Treasonable Offences Decree No 29 of 1993'. The tribunal, according to him, was empowered to try military officers as well as civilians who were not subject to military laws but had committed coup-related offences. After that, he read out the names of the tribunal members and asked, 'Do you have any objection to the participation of any of the members in your trial? If you have, the tribunal would make a replacement'.

'No. No.', I answered.

He introduced all members of the prosecution and the defense. The government had nominated lawyers, he said, to defend the accused but if the accused wanted to engage any lawyer not short-listed by the government he was free to do so. I turned down that offer as well. In retrospect, I believe that was an error. I should have objected politely to the members of the tribunal and their choice of a lawyer for me. I should have objected to being tried by that tribunal. Not that it would have made any significant difference, but it would have been a good way to say: stop this nonsense. I regret missing that opportunity.

Aziza read what amounted to a one-count charge against me.

'That in Lagos you caused to be published in the May 29 edition of The*NEWS* magazine a story captioned *Not Guilty: Army Panel Clears Coup Suspects*, a story which was capable of inciting the public against the government.'

So these inquisitors are saying that we are heretics of their own concept of peace and transgressors against their criminal order. It is just as well. I thought.

He spelt out the particulars of the offence.

'That the said story portrays the arrest and trials of the coup plotters as mere witch-hunting and this is capable of causing disgruntlement among members of the armed forces,' he went on.

'Because the intention of the story is to set the coup plotters free, you are hereby charged with treason, as an accessory after the fact of treason, an offence punishable under the Treason and Treasonable Offences Decree No.29 of 1993. Are you guilty or not guilty?'

Again that made me ponder: an accessory after the fact is a person who, knowing that a crime has been committed, aids or shelters the offender with the intent to defeat justice. That's how *Webster's Dictionary of English Language* defines it. *Now, have these toadies been able to prove that an offence has been committed? If this story can truly prevent Abacha from killing the innocent, let it be.* I said: 'Not guilty at all'.

The tribunal rose for recess, perhaps to allow the prosecution and the defense to prepare adequately for the battle, the

winner of which was already decided. In the intervening minutes I met, for the first time, the defense attorney whom the
government had picked for me: a tall, dark and sullen Lieutenant-Colonel. The officer took my credentials and said, 'I think
this thing is so clear. The copy of the magazine is here as evidence of what you did. This case would be a lot easier for us to
handle if you plead guilty…'

In anger I cut him short.

'Plead guilty? Why should I plead guilty? No, I won't plead
guilty. What gives them the idea that I was the one who edited
this edition of the magazine? Do they know my style of editing?
Anyway, I know that no matter the strength or weakness of my
defence in this court I will not be acquitted.' The attorney told
me to calm down.

Of course, I was convinced in my mind that it did not matter
whether I edited the magazine or not.

K-O-O-M! K-O-O-O-M! K-O-O-O-O-M! COU-OU-
OU-R-T!

We all stood up. The court was back in session. The lapdog
judge made another slight bow. 'Be seated', he said. He tested
the microphone again. I heard him breathing.

'Is the prosecution now ready to open its case?', Aziza said.

'Yes, m'lord.

A lawyer on the prosecution then invited me to the dock.
The file that I had seen at the SIP was before him. But as he
was about to start his cross-examination, the judge interrupted
him,

'Mr. Ajibade, the tribunal has decided to give you a chance
to say a few words before the prosecution opens its case.'

I was not expecting that. I suddenly had a hunch that the
tribunal wanted me to play the biblical Stephen. In the *Good
News Bible,* I had read that when he was dragged before a

council similar to Aziza's, Stephen was asked a simple question about the cause of which he was an untiring defender. Replying, Stephen, a man blessed with oratorical powers, delivered a lengthy and passionate speech. He launched a frontal attack, hitting the members of the council and the tyrannical king they were working for, with stinging words. They sat through it all, seething with rage. When he was done, they bundled him out of the city and stoned him to death.

I knew that the eloquence of Demosthenes, even if I had that gift, would not get me released. It did not even seem prudent for me to vent my fury openly as I addressed the tribunal:

'I have nothing lengthy to say to this tribunal. Since this is a treason trial, more or less, a matter of life-and-death, I want your tribunal to prove the charge against me beyond all reasonable doubt. Is the story for which I'm under trial true or false? In what way has the story published in May, for which I'm being tried in July, incited Nigerians against the government? In what way has the same story caused disharmony within the military? If you prove this beyond all reasonable doubt, I will accept your verdict in good faith. Thank you.'

The spotlight was warm, but the court was chilly.

'The prosecution can now proceed with its case', Aziza said.

'Thank you, m'lord. If it is true Mr. Ajibade that you did not edit this particular edition of *TheNEWS*, how come your name is printed here as the editor?'

'A technical error.'

'Was there a meeting at which you were removed as the editor of the magazine?'

'Yes, there was.'

'Was the decision a majority decision?'

'Yes, it was.'

'When your name was not removed as the editor on the

imprint did you complain?'

'I did.'

'Why is your name still here as the editor?'

The predictable waffle of Lieutenant Oguntayo began to irritate me. He obviously wanted to discredit my evidence. *Why was the tribunal interested in this, not whether the story was true or false?*

'Look…Look, I've told you why just now. Go out there and buy the latest edition of *TheNEWS*. Maybe it still bears my imprint. Does that mean I edited the magazine in my place of confinement?'

Pleased that he had made me angry, Oguntayo took the magazine to Aziza who examined it and accepted it as exhibit 1.

'M'lord, permit me to read the entire story to the hearing of the court.'

'Permission granted.'

As he read the story he placed emphasis on some of the juicier passages, measured vitriol, dripping from it.

'M'lord, permit me to enter my witness.'

'Permission granted.'

The prosecution then brought in an army officer, PW1, who, under oath, testified:

'I am an avid reader of *TheNEWS* magazine. When I read the copy of *TheNEWS* in question I felt so bad because it paints the coup plot incident as a hoax. It is as if the magazine holds a strong belief that the government is a liar. I believe this is not true, sir.' I was irritated by this fellow's pious civility.

The prosecutor asked his PW1 to leave.

'Permit me, m'lord, to produce my second exhibit'

'Permission granted'

'Take a look at this. Are you the author?

'Yes.'

'Where did you write it?'

'At the DMI.'

'Where you were being detained?'

'Yes.'

'Permit me m'lord to read the story.'

'Permission granted.'

He read one of the stories which the DMI had intercepted and then took it to the salivating judge who amusingly swooped down on it like a hungry vulture.

'Exhibit admitted as exhibit 2.'

'I put it to you, Mr. Ajibade, that you're an incorrigible offender. On that note m'lord I rest my case.'

Stony silence.

Is this what the law of evidence is all about? I asked myself. *If criminal law were as easy as this, everybody would become a lawyer. If this is truly what the law of evidence is about any accused will either be automatically free or pronounced guilty depending on the mood and politics in the land, or the temperament and bias of the judge.* I stayed calm as I remembered that it was a farce. But it was the peculiar calmness of a cow that is about to be slaughtered.

The linchpin in the presentation of 'my lawyer' was what I had modestly proposed as a layman. He added nothing significant. The legal sparring, the trading of verbal tackles that I would have loved to see was denied the court by my government-appointed lawyer, this Lawyer-do-nothing.

'Tomorrow both the defense and prosecution shall make their final submissions. We shall also listen to the presentation of the Judge-Advocate and the tribunal will deliver its judgement.'

That was Aziza rounding off my first appearance at the tribunal. I went after 'my lawyer' to express my displeasure at the way he let the prosecutor to have his way.

'I don't find the way you handled it funny. Even in the Law of Moses at least two witnesses are required to establish *a prima facie* case. The prosecutor produced just one witness, an army officer who purportedly represented all the Nigerians whom my publication incited, and you did not raise an objection. It's amazing. In a treason trial you never said a word to contradict anything. I know you people *are all together*, but you should have done your legal profession some good, at least.'

He promised that the following day would be better. But July 29, 1995 was worse. When he came to greet me in the waiting room, I asked him, just for my own record, to give me short profiles of all the lawyers on the prosecution. I thought he had gone to bring the list when he left me. The man returned instead with soldiers. The officer- in-charge, his mouth full of froth, asked me to repeat what I had requested from 'my lawyer'. I did. And what followed was a rebuke.

'You are in one big problem. You still want to create another one for yourself. You like problem too much, *fa*. What's your problem?'

He and his soldiers left like some exuberant, super-charged bulldogs. I felt an unsullied disgust for 'my lawyer', who told me I should not worry, that the incident would not affect my case. I was still contemplating that when a Steyr truck brought Dr. Beko Ransome-Kuti to the tribunal in handcuffs. He clutched a small bottle of water in his chained hands, and his two breast pockets contained two packets of Gold Leaf cigarettes and a lighter. Commander L.M.O. Fabiyi, Mbah and I stood up in honour of the man who was looking grave in his gray safari suit as he was led to the waiting room. Surprisingly, the soldiers, too, followed suit. He sat next to me and I briefed him about the game of the absurd in the court of Aziza. Ransome-Kuti replied so gently, 'If you're expecting life imprisonment, I'm sure mine would be death by firing squad. What a country! What a life!'

As soon as he began to smoke, Sergeant Bob Zome cautioned that he did not like people smoking in his territory. Ransome-Kuti looked at him, smiled and said,

'This is not your territory. This territory belongs to Nigeria'.

He briefed me on the efforts the Campaign for Democracy (CD) had made to get us released, not knowing that the same fate would befall him. The tribunal, soon after that, sent a soldier who led me back to its court.

The court clerk once again banged the table thrice and shouted COU-OU-OU-R-T!

We all stood up. The jaded actor in the role of judge entered on a stride of false dignity.

'In the case of the State vs Mr. Kunle Ajibade, the tribunal will now hear the final submission of the prosecution'.

'M'lord', Oguntayo pleaded, 'before I do that, may it please the court to let me announce the appearance of my second witness'.

I felt betrayed as my mind went to the suggestion I had made the previous day. The impatient tribunal was very irritated because the case had been closed. But, nevertheless, it allowed the prosecutor to bring in a naval officer who, without any variation, repeated what the first witness had said.

The prosecution summed up its presentation, saying that a written document was more valid in law than oral evidence. He cited some legal authorities to back that up. Since my name was on the masthead, the magazine could not have been edited by any other person and that 'based on the evidence adduced, the accused is guilty as charged and should be convicted.' He said I was a dangerous criminal who should not be allowed to roam the streets of Nigeria because I would commit more crimes.

Me, a dangerous criminal?

The submission of the defense counsel, when he was asked to round off, was very tepid. He repeated his old lines: that the tribunal had not proved that I edited the magazine. Since he did not cross examine the witnesses brought by the prosecution, I concluded that the lawyer had become a mere spectator, a defense counsel that had to go against his client's wishes.

The Judge-Advocate, Lieutenant-Colonel Nathaniel Madza, then read what was supposed to be, in the main, legal advice to Aziza, who was not a lawyer. After summarising the submissions of both the prosecution and the defence, he said:

'The critical point now is not whether Ajibade edited the magazine or not. So long as he belongs to the executive cadre of the organisation that published *TheNEWS*, he should be held liable for the misdemeanors of the said magazine. This is what is called vicarious responsibility'. *Is this what the law says, or just Madza's bullshit? I thought.* The Judge-Advocate continued, 'The tribunal should not bother itself with proving the case beyond all reasonable doubt but beyond all iota of doubt'. *My guilt was already predetermined.*

His lordship announced,

'The court now retires into chambers to consider its judgement'. *Into chambers? Which chambers?*

As I sat on the wooden bench in the court, I heard the *eminent jurists* in chambers laughing out loud. When the lawyer carefully chosen by the government to defend me came to ask for my dependents as he would enter a mitigation plea, I sensed that the *hour of evil foretold* was most imminent.

Suddenly.

The usual bang on the table followed by a shout of COU-OU-OU-R-T!

We all stood up. His Omnipotence the judge entered, this

time without a file; he only brought a sheet of paper, judgement written on it.

'Be seated'

Grave silence.

The judge began to read his text. He gave a good summary of the proceedings, noting every point advanced and the exhibit tendered. The tribunal, he said, had been very *meticulous* in the manner the trial was conducted.

'Any mitigation plea on behalf of the accused?', he asked after a short pause.

My government-appointed lawyer told the court, yes my lord, and then rose to appeal to the tribunal to temper justice with mercy 'because the accused is the chief bread-winner in his family.'

Menacing silence.

The judge gave his ruling.

'The tribunal has considered very seriously the mitigation plea of the defense. But the law must take its course. Ajibade is found guilty as charged. The accused is hereby condemned to life imprisonment.'

K-O-O-M! K-O-O-O-M! K-O-O-O-O-M! COU-OU—R-T!

The emissary of Abacha thereupon went away, content with a duty accomplished. The other members of the tribunal, who had scarcely uttered a word during the trial, followed him, hopping like a flock of kangaroos. Under Aziza, justice abandoned its honourable and exalted position and descended to a dirty arena of an interested party. I believed this case would have been different if I had appeared before the incorruptible Justice Kayode Eso, or Justice Chukwudifu Oputa, who drew a line between the *rule of man* and the *rule of law,* and voted only for *the rule of law*.

Within seconds, I was led into the waiting truck. Hemmed in by several armed soldiers, I was driven back lickety-split to the Military Hospital, Ikoyi. But in spite of their overzealous quarantine, I went to the bathroom with the wrap of my toilet tissue and my pen hidden in my underwear. I put on the shower as I perched in one corner to write a couple of short notes to my wife and colleagues about my encounter with the obscene court of Aziza where idiocy contended with absurdity, and both came up winners.

Waking up in the hospital the next day, I ruminated over the judgement pronounced on me. I told myself that if Abacha got away with this, he would frame more people. He would also kill more people. Faced with the grim reality of being dumped in jail, the brave face I had put on started to wane.

Even though I had never been in prison in the course of my duty as a journalist, I had a fair idea, through my readings, that prison is like a tomb of the living-dead anywhere in the world. If Nigeria on the outside was a house of horror, I could imagine that its jailhouse would be life- denying. I thought that it was a lot of relief that I succeeded in saving my colleagues from going to jail, but was their freedom not a qualified one with me in prison? I found myself thinking momentarily of ways of escape.

I thought also about the perils of my profession. In the May 1904 issue of the *North American Review* magazine, Joseph Pulitzer argued pointedly and robustly about the privilege of journalism: 'The journalist', he said, 'has a position that is all his own. He alone has the privilege of moulding the opinion, touching the hearts and appealing to the reason of hundreds of thousands every day. Here is the most fascinating of all professions. The soldier may wait forty years for his opportunity. Most lawyers, most physicians, most clergymen die in obscurity, but every single day opens new doors for the journalist who holds the confidence of the community and has the capacity to address it'.

What Pulitzer did not say is that there is a sense in which the privilege of journalism could become a yoke, for it is this same privilege that a dictator desires to have: the capacity to control reason, the capacity to reinvent and affect other people's thinking. This explains why there is always tension between the good press and the totalitarian state. It made me wonder in those gloomy moments whether journalism can ever be free of repression, whether the attack on the right to inform people can ever stop, in spite of the liberal recognition of journalists by our constitution which imposes on the press the obligation to provide a responsible information service in the public intrest. As we had proved, the press, incredibly, can report the news under extremely difficult circumstances at great personal risk, but can words alone bring down the tyrant?

My arrest, interrogation and subsequent imprisonment were part of a stream of history of press repression in my country, whenever journalism ran into conflict with arbitrary or arrogant power. Since the establishment of the first Nigerian newspaper, *Iwe Irohin,* in Abeokuta by Reverend Henry Townsend, in 1859, political authorities had always tried to muzzle the press. The British colonial lords were very suspicious of journalist-freedom fighters like Herbert Macaulay, Nnamdi Azikiwe, Obafemi Awolowo, Ladoke Akintola, Anthony Enahoro, H.O. Davies, Abubakar Imam and a few others. Indeed, as punishment, Davies, Mokwugo Okoye and Herbert Macaulay were imprisoned on different occasions for different reasons not unconnected with their polemical writings.

Before we were *jailed for life*, there were those television journalists in Ibadan, who were ordered to be caned by Colonel Adeyinka Adebayo, then military governor of Western State, for covering a party he was attending in the late 1960s, contrary to an earlier directive he gave. According to Wole Soyinka in *The Man Died*, the wound of Segun Sowemimo, one of the journalists, was badly infected and soon his lungs were impaired. He was flown to England subsequently where one of his legs was amputated. But that did not help matters. Sowemimo died.

Before our tribulation, there was Minere Amakiri, the Port Harcourt correspondent of the *Nigerian Observer,* who was not only given a hair cut with a rusty blade, but was also stripped naked and given 24 strokes of the cane on his back for writing a story about the impending teachers strike when the then governor of Rivers State, Navy Commander Alfred Diete-Spiff, was celebrating his 31st birthday in 1973. Four years later, Chris Okolie's magazine, *Newbreed,* was proscribed by the regime of Obasanjo because, according to Obasanjo in his Dodan Barracks memoirs, *Not My Will,* the publisher refused to spike a story on the NSO. However, Okolie insisted that his magazine was banned for criticising the Obasanjo regime.

Before the ordeals of the four innocent journalists, Anyanwu, Mbah, Charles-Obi and myself, who were now jailed for life, there were Tunde Thompson and Nduka Irabor of *The Guardian* who were jailed for one year in 1985 over a story on foreign posting which offended the regime of Buhari. They were the victims of Decree No 4 of 1985, which made it an offence to publish anything that embarrassed a government official.

Before our case, Chris Mammah of *The Punch*, Onoise Osunbor of *African Concord,* and Chris Okojie of *Vanguard* were arrested in the wake of the Gideon Orkar Coup in 1990 for allegedly associating in the past with some of the officers involved. They were only lucky to be released early.

Before our incarceration, Alifa Daniel, who was the *National Concord* correspondent in Kogi State was, in 1992, bathed in acid by people suspected to be the agents of the State government because of his anti-government reports.

Before this trial, some of my colleagues had, on March 12, 1993, been on trial at Justice Moshood Olugbani's Court 10, Igbosere, Lagos. About thirty lawyers volunteered to defend them. The lawyers included Chief Gani Fawehinmi, Dr. Olu Onagorowa, Kanmi Ishola Osobu, Falana, Professor Itse Sagay, Mike Ozekhome and Layi Babatunde. The judge told the jeering crowd in his court that he had ordered the arrest of Onanuga, Olorunyomi, Kehinde and Adesokan, the previous day as an administrative procedure to ensure that they did not disappear.

But Fawehinmi disagreed, saying that Olugbani did so because the journalists 'did a cover story on you and you are not happy. You are showing bitterness. You hold that grudge against them and that is why you want to send them to prison without hearing a word from their counsel. It is not right. The law and God will not allow it. It is not fair'.

Justice Olugbani said that was not true: he had not read the story we had done on his high-handedness and the allegation of corruption against him*. Because of the altercations which ensued, I remember that the late Osobu rose to caution Olugbani. 'The legal temperature is rising', he observed. 'In the time of Justice J.I.C. Taylor, who once presided in this court, things never got out of hand'. As soon as Falana got up to introduce himself as Chiedu Ezeanah's lawyer and a friend of the court, the judge shouted him down: 'Who asked you to speak? Don't be my friend. I don't need you.' Flaming with anger, the judge sent the journalists to Ikoyi Prison to be remanded there till

---

* Justice Moshood Olugbani was retired by the National Judicial Council (NJC) from the Lagos State Judiciary in 2002 for curruption.

March 19, 1993.

We were in the court in respect of a story, which we called *Dirty Humphrey*. The cover had revealed some shady deals involving Professor Humphrey Nwosu, the then Chairman of National Electoral Commission. Nwosu would soon go down in Nigerian contemporary history as the man who was not bold enough to announce the results of the June 12 presidential election that was widely acclaimed as free and fair.

Lord Denning, the much-respected British Judge, says in his November 20, 1980 Richard Dimbleby Lecture, *Misuse of Power*, that 'Every judge on his appointment discards all politics and all prejudices'. I was truly baffled as I watched this High Court judge spew so much venom without any compunction. But the self-importance of that court at least was grounded in some democratic posturing unlike Aziza's.

The siege on the right of the journalists to chronicle events was bolstered by draconian decrees. Yet Section 21 of the 1979 Constitution states: 'The press, radio, television and other agencies of the mass media shall at all times be free to uphold the fundamental objectives contained in this chapter and uphold the responsibility and accountability of the Government to the people.'

In a largely oral society like our own, where poverty and illiteracy conspire against the intellect, journalism is also faced with a gloomy prospect. But if there is no good journalism that calls all irresponsible leaders to proper accounting, the downtrodden would not have any hope. I know that the public good served by honest reporting makes journalism a worthwhile profession. I also know that those who give up on seeking for justice always end up as citizens in the gutter. Journalism is a dangerous job. I accept its special risks and obligations. I accept its problems and possibilities.

I remembered that before this phantom coup, there had been other bloody coups. The most well known being the January 15, 1966 Chukwuma Nzeogwu coup in which 12 Nigerians including the Prime Minister, Sir Abubakar Tafawa Balewa; Premier of the North, Alhaji Ahmadu Bello; Premier of the West, Chief Ladoke Akintola, were murdered; the July 29, 1966 Theophilus Danjuma revenge coup in which 13 Nigerians including Major- General J.T. U. Aguiyi-Ironsi and Lieutenant-Colonel Adekunle Fajuyi were murdered; the February 13, 1976 Dimka coup in which the Head of State, General Murtala Muhammed and Lieutenant-Colonel Ibrahim Taiwo, among others, were killed, and for which 39 Nigerians were publicly executed; the 1986 Vatsa coup for which 10 senior officers lost their lives; the 1990 Orkar coup for which 68 people were killed.

Going by what I witnessed at the SMT, I began to doubt whether the majority of the officers killed for coup related offences in the past were actually guilty. With the benefit of my experience, I reckoned that all the grand plans supposedly made by the coupists were usually mere propaganda.

The Aziza tribunal had no concrete evidence of coup plotting against more than forty Nigerians who went through its grill. It based its judgement on hearsay allegations and circumstantial evidence. Out of frustration, and in its bewildering twisted logic, it accused the officers and soldiers before it of *constructive conspiracy* to conceal their plot, which, to the tribunal, was a more serious offence. It turned out that the majority of the officers condemned to death or jailed by the tribunal had disagreed in the past with Abacha.

Obasanjo, for instance, was accused and jailed because he would not support the regime. Soon after the ING of Shonekan was declared illegal in 1993 by a Lagos High Court, Abacha invited Obasanjo to his official home in Lagos and asked him, *what do we do with this?* He wanted Obasanjo to say, *take over*. Instead, Obasanjo said that Nigeria was fed up with military government and the international community would not tolerate it.

When the Arewa House in Kaduna invited Obasanjo to give the keynote address at the conference on 'State of the Nation: Which Way Forward?, in the first week of February 1994, the regime of Abacha sent a presidential plane to fly Obasanjo to Kaduna via Abuja. At a meeting he had with Abacha, he was told to use the opportunity to speak well of the regime. More than that, Abacha appealed to Obasanjo to use his international profile to sell his administration abroad. Obasanjo then asked for a programme that he could sell but Abacha had none.

Not satisfied with the outcome of the meeting, Abacha called Gwadabe, then his Principal Staff Officer (PSO), whose idea it was to bring Obasanjo to Abuja, and warned him that he should stop pressurising him into meetings with people like Obasanjo. He told Gwadabe that Obasanjo had been one of the senior officers who had sent him (Abacha) to Chad, expecting that he would die there.

Obasanjo, in his address, said that the government of Abacha was not sincere:

> 'If a government, out of lack of confidence in itself, fails to repose confidence in us by telling us its programme and how long it requires to implement that programme, why should such a government ask for our confidence and understanding? And if it does, why should we give it? After all, confidence begets

confidence... And how seriously should anybody take the idea that the Constitutional Conference that has no say in voting in a Military Government should determine its agenda? For us to take such an idea seriously, the outcome of the decision of the Constitutional Conference should be binding on the Military Government... But the greatest danger that military government poses to our polity is not the perpetuation of economic and social mismanagement, bad as this is. The greatest danger lies in the failure of the military to break the vicious cycle of succeeding itself. Unless Nigerians stand up against this trend, it may continue indefinitely.'*

Abacha was not happy with that address. The SSS was asked to trail Obasanjo who was then the chair of National Unity Organisation (NUO). The report it submitted about a meeting Obasanjo held with other Nigerians on the state of the nation was not enough to nail him for a coup. So Bello-Fadile was tortured to implicate him. Bello-Fadile told the SIP that he met Obasanjo in his farm to discuss a coup.

But after the tribunal had sentenced Obasanjo to life imprisonment, Bello-Fadile wrote him this note:

> '*I was put under unbearable threats to my life by torture and other dehumanising treatment during the investigation. Noting that I have a first degree heart blockade that has put me on daily medication for the past ten years; and realising that a heart attack could be induced under the situation and end my life, I had no option but to succumb to the whims of the interrogators and make the statements they wanted about you and General Shehu Yar'Adua. I had hoped for a fair trial under the law, which would have cleared all of us. Sir, the rest of the story you know and it is better left for posterity. There-*

---

* *The Guardian*, February 4 & 7, 1994

fore, sir, it is my wish and personal desire (to bor-
row your words spoken some 20 years ago when I
was a Second Lieutenant) that you accept your cur-
rent situation as your further contribution to de-
mocracy on a strong footing in the country where
our children can live in peace and freedom without
fear. As my former Commander-in-Chief, accept me
*like the Biblical prodigal son.'**

Obasanjo's reply was terse: *'If God forgives me my sins,*
who am I not to forgive anybody who asks me for forgive-
ness. But forgiveness is of God and you should ask God for
forgiveness'.

The case of Major-General Shehu Musa Yar'Adua was similar to Obasanjo's. As a member of the Constitutional Conference, he engineered a motion that gave the military up to 1996
to leave. The Abacha regime thought that Yar'Adua wanted to
oppose its government with his political machine, Peoples
Democratic Movement (PDM). Abacha did not set up the Constitutional Conference to send his regime out of office: it was to
buy time for the government that seized power. To that extent,
there were many government nominees, and the conferees were
specifically told that the issue of *June 12* was a no-go area.
Some of the conferees said that their mandate was greater than
the mandate of the winner of the annulled presidential election
results. Chief Emeka Odumegwu-Ojukwu, the former leader
of the failed Republic of Biafra, was the unelected spokesman
of that group. Umaru Dikko, a top member of the National
Party of Nigeria (NPN) in charge of the notorious Presidential
Rice Task Force, said the North would go to war if *June 12*
election result was de-annulled.

But Yar'Adua, who was the Chief of Staff Supreme Head-

---

* From *"The Country of Anything Goes"* by Olusegun Obasanjo, *The New York Review* September
24, 1998.

quarters in the Obasanjo military administration of 1976-1979, went behind the scenes to empower the Conference to rise, almost in one accord, to give the military its marching orders. *Go, Abacha, in 1996!** .

Responding, a jittery Abacha put all his military Commanders on red alert. For instance, in the Danjuma Hall the following day, the Commandant of the Command and Staff College, Jaji, Kaduna, Major-General Unimna, who was also a member of the Provisional Ruling Council (PRC), called an assembly of both the senior and junior divisions of the school and told them to be very vigilant because the decision of the Constitutional Conference (which, according to him, had temporarily been hijacked) was an indication of a deep hatred for the military, and members of the armed forces should not allow themselves to be treated with ignominy.

The conference, which took that far-reaching decision, was sent on a long recess with immediate effect. By the time it came back, the majority of the members were singing a different tune. The Constitutional Conference that many Nigerians were praising for a good decision suddenly reversed itself. Abacha did not forgive Yar'Adua for the embarrassment that decision caused his fledgling government. The whiplash of Abacha's fear was only accentuated by other political moves by Yar'Adua. It was merely a matter of time, therefore, before he would have another brush with the tyrant.

W hen coup plotting became an important national project for Abacha in the early part of 1995, Aziza was not the

---

* Yar'Adua, an aristocrat from Katsina, considered Abacha a lowly upstart. Because he had a personal disagreement with the winner of the annulled June 12 election, he was not interested in it being de-annulled. He wanted a fresh election which he hoped to win.

first officer considered fit to head the SMT. The first choice was Major-General Musa Bamaiyi of the National Drug Law Enforcement Agency (NDLEA). But Bamaiyi reportedly went into hiding when he heard the news from the grapevine. He distanced himself from what he told some of his confidants would turn out to be a dangerous assignment.

Aziza grabbed the job. Somersaulting in the web of opportunism, he forgot that if time devours other things he did as an officer, it would not swallow the memories of his crooked trial and sick verdict.

SEVEN

~~~~~~

In the House
of Cruelties

Leaving the hospital was emotional. That morning in the company of Dr. Nwachukwu and Mrs. Bamidele, a senior nurse, Dr. Fisher said:

'We will abide by your preference to go back to the Security Group today. In your discharge paper we've written that you should be brought back in two weeks for a check-up. We're insisting that the test should not be done in any other place but here. You are not leaving here to go and die; you're leaving to live...'

I was close to tears. I thanked them for their genuine concern. As soon as they left, my mind concentrated on the dark song of resentment which my compatriots were singing: *How long will this nightmare last, this season of overwhelming melancholy, this thick darkness around us?* I did not know.

Thirty minutes later, the soldiers from the Security Group brought their chains. They shackled me and led me to their truck. *All those who are distorting the system, will they go scot-free?* The stream of my reveries and remembrances kept galloping like the roomy truck I was in.

The Security Group is nestled in the marshy area of Apapa in Lagos. Enclosed by high walls of concrete capped with wire mesh of the tangled thorn variety, it is surrounded by the living quarters of some of its officers. This is where the system tries to purge people of imaginary mutiny; this is a place where the armed men are very resistant to compassion. Whenever evil hours befall Nigeria, and tyrants grab what is valuable to us and smash it against the granite, the officers here make some quick gains from the massive funds set aside to nurture the climate of fear. If the officers here were asked to shoot their mothers for money and power, I think they would gladly do so.

Months before we were confined in the Security Group, hostility broke out between Bamaiyi of the NDLEA and Olu because a cocaine pusher, fettered and pushed inside the underground cell, escaped after he had bought his freedom. Yet there is no other place in Nigeria where you have a dungeon like the one here: it has eight cells, each of them spacious enough to take a two by six mattress; it has its own bathroom and toilet; a sitting room with a ceiling fan. The main lock-up has a similar structure as the underground one except that it has ten cells. Because the place was crammed with detainees when we were there, offices of its desk officers were converted into cells. I was detained in one of those offices.

But Shehu Sani was locked up in a real cell. Until his arrest on March 9, 1995 in Kaduna, Sani was the National Vice-Chairman of the Campaign for Democracy. He and his colleagues were campaigning to arouse the sleeping consciousness of the largely illiterate citizens in Northern Nigeria who had been run down by feudalism. He knew that this path was delicate to walk. Was Dr. Bala Mohammed not killed in his house in Kano because he was opposed to feudalism? Did Mahmmud Tukur, the radical historian not die in mysterious circumstance?

The SSS brought Sani to Lagos and locked him up in Maximum Security Prison, Kirikiri. On July 1, 1995, he was charged with managing an unlawful society, an offence punishable under section 63 of the Criminal Code. For this he was jailed for seven years by the tribunal.

He was again brought back to the tribunal only to be convicted and sentenced to life imprisonment on July 14, 1995 as an accessory after the fact of treason because he had written a note to Ransome-Kuti from prison, informing him that he had been taken to the Aziza SMT which he described as a kangaroo court.

'You see, by putting some of you in the offices of my staff, we're giving you the best we could offer. Honestly, you need to see where people are detained at the Intercentre. Oh, I don't want you to be there, particularly you civilians who will soon go home. Cheers. All the best.'

With that remark Olu finally admitted me to the Security Group after I had stayed for three nights in the waiting room. In the interval, his telephone purred.

'Do you speak Hausa?' he asked.

'No,' I replied.

He chatted endlessly in impeccable Hausa, punctuating many sentences with *walahitalah*i. Olu was given to deadly intrigues. He would order the arrest of someone, ask his soldiers to put the victim in chains and feign ignorance of the incident.

'Oh, the man is already here. Why are you still putting him in chains?'

I was that man. But his officers and soldiers understood complaints like that to mean: thank you for a good job!

'I will speak to my director about the barium meal test. We shall do something positive very soon.'

My bad reputation in the Security Group preceded my arrival. All because of the intercepted stories. But I was lucky to have suffered an attack of malaria on two of the nights I had stayed in the waiting room. I was in bad shape the day Olu finally made up his mind to put me up in the same cell with Ransome-Kuti. It was a qualified allowance. I was one of the detainees in the Security Group who were prohibited from having any contact with anyone on the outside including Bunmi, my wife.

'You see, Ajibade, the letter of Ransome-Kuti for visitation is now with the DMI. We want to finish with that before we consider your own. Please, bear with us. Cheers. All the best.'

The week they allowed Morenike Ransome-Kuti, after a lot of hurdles, to see her father, I thought they would begin to process my application for visit, but something else happened. *A.M.NEWS* carried a banner story that Ransome-Kuti was critically ill in detention. Who was responsible for that story?

I was, but the Security Group never knew.

Ransome-Kuti and I were summoned by the Commanding Officer of the Security Group to a meeting with his officers. Pointing an accusing finger at Morenike, who just visited her father, he said the paper was very wrong: 'Ransome-Kuti is ill, yes, but not critically ill.' It was an attempt to cancel the visitation right earlier granted to Ransome-Kuti. Mine, of course, had been ruled out completely. Ransome-Kuti valiantly defended his daughter, asking: how could she have been responsible for the story in which she was not mentioned?

'Now that the story is out already, would it be out of place to send a rejoinder to *A.M.NEWS*?', I suggested.

A resounding no was all I got in reply.

Because I was not allowed to make contact with my family, I would have starved if Queenette Lewis-Allagoa and Anyanwu had not shared their food with me. Lewis-Allagoa, one of Gwadabe's friends, was the woman the government initially wanted to use to implicate Gwadabe. But, against intense pressure, she refused to play ball, which was why she was jailed.

As we lay waiting for the final decision of the PRC, the rumour mill was agog over several versions of the prison terms which Abacha was going to announce in his October broadcast. At a point, there was speculation that I would bag twenty-five years. Initially that did not worry me because many of us still believed that Abacha would back off in the face of intense pressures.

But the murder of Papa Alfred Rewane on October 6, 1995 by people suspected to be agents of government changed all that. The old man was gunned down by the assassins in his bedroom. The unsullied image of Papa Rewane loomed large, not just as a financier of the Action Group, the UPN and NADECO but as a dogged fighter for social justice in Nigeria. Any time he felt that matters had gone beyond granting press interviews, he would pay for insertions in newspapers to express his views in some comprehensive form, not as a rabble-rouser, but as a deeply concerned citizen and a patriarch of democratic struggle. That assassination, to me, then, in the Security Group, was an ominous sign that we were now in a state of blood. Horrible realities would soon lend credence to that presentiment. *Why do bad people prosper and the good ones crushed?* I wondered, after hearing the news of his assassination.

We relieved the tedium of waiting with reading, playing in door games and praying to God to deliver the country. Hope animated us. Staying in the same room, sleeping on the same dirty mattress* with Ransome-Kuti was quirky, yet socially and intellectually stimulating. Our clothes and mattress were soaked in sweat each morning because the heat in the room was so intense, and intolerable.

Before I was brought to join them in the Security Group, he was condemned to solitary confinement. The Commander had given an order that he should be locked up except to eat, smoke, or use the toilet. The order was followed to the letter but because Ransome-Kuti was a chain-smoker, he would call the attention of the Sergeant on duty many times only to say, *I want to smoke*. They later gave him the liberty to keep his Gold Leaf cigarettes.

Chess and cigarettes were two of his unquenchable passions. Waking up in the morning, the first sign that he was awake was lighting a stick of cigarette. As a non-smoker, I had to put up with the smoke and stench of his tobacco. For that he had no apology. After smoking, he would make some moves on his chessboard. As he played against himself, he would talk and laugh with an imaginary opponent, his invisible but apparently not invincible adversary.

For Ransome-Kuti, I suppose, chess was not just a diversion; it was a kind of noble preoccupation itself. He gave me my first serious lesson in chess but because I had set for myself a reading deadline, I was not a diligent pupil. Austere in nature, he ate frugal meals and dressed simply. He was even mindful of his balance sheet in detention. His has been a life of conscientious parsimony — a lesson in prudence.

In him, you have the virtue and the vice of the illustrious family of Reverend I.O. Ransome-Kuti concentrated in equal proportion. He shares the sobriety of Professor Olikoye Ransome-Kuti and the eccentricity of (Olu)Fela Anikulapo-Kuti. The resemblance between the brothers is not particularly exact, but

---

* Until Colonel Sabo Mohammed ordered that a new bed, bedspread and mattress should be bought for him.

there is a community of features between them, which reminds one of Mrs. Funmilayo Ransome-Kuti, their mother, a fearless Nigerian nationalist, whose organisation, Abeokuta Women's Union, fought for the rights of women to vote. Described in 1947 by the *West African Pilot* as the Lioness of Lisabi, Mrs. Ransome-Kuti also led those Egba women on a campaign against arbitrary taxation of women. Indeed, that struggle led to the abdication of Oba Ademola II in 1949. It was a local coup against a local tyrant and his colonial masters.

The event that submerged Mrs. Ransome-Kuti in deep depression, which eventually led to her death in 1978, happened on February 18, 1977. Segun Ademola, who was an employee of the Africa 70 Organisation Limited owned by Fela, had a disagreement with a military traffic policeman who impounded the car he was driving at the Ojuelegba junction of the Agege Motor Road. He was accused of committing a traffic offence. Ransome-Kuti, who told me this story, stated in one of his petitions on the subject: 'A little while after this disagreement, hundreds of fully armed soldiers from Abalti Barracks, Ojuelegba, led by one Major Dauda marched on and surrounded our family house at 14A, Agege Motor Road, Idi-Oro, Lagos. When they left five hours later, the whole premises had been razed to the ground by fire set by the soldiers. Besides the storey building, they also burnt my clinic, which was located in the premises and looted property, raped women and physically assaulted scores of residents, visitors and passers-by. A total of 55 people were treated in hospital for various injuries ranging from lacerations, burns to broken bones'.

In a magazine advertorial*, Major Mustapha H. Jokolo, who is now the Emir of Gwandu, confessed that the then Chief of Army Staff, General Theophilus Yakubu Danjuma, gave the

---

* *Citizen* magazine, November 9, 1992

order that Fela be brought to him dead or alive. The family had petitioned the Head of State, Obasanjo, whose government compounded the problem by seizing the land of the family and that of its neighbours without paying any compensation. The judiciary, too, did not help matters. Sitting at the Lagos High Court, Justice L.J. Dosunmu dismissed the case, saying, 'the king can do no wrong'.

This pathetic incident did not stop Ransome-Kuti from campaigning for the release of Obasanjo from detention until he too was arrested. That would have run against the grain of someone who grew up in a family of activists and campaigners.

To him anything that is not practical is nothing. Try to establish any issue in theoretical terms with him and you will incur his wrath. Try to point out some conflicting impulses that coexist within him, he would ask you, *How?* Even when you've made yourself clear enough.

His quest on the Nigerian political terrain has been for one major purpose: pressurising those in power to do what is right. In a country of so many vile politicians, who love the benefits of power and prestige of office, and not its responsibilities; in a nation of rulers who declare war against integrity, citizens like him will always step on toes. That's why he had suffered detention on several occasions.

Yet he showed no sign of disillusionment. He did not budge. He was not tired. At the SIP, they wanted to know how he got the Bello-Fadile's defence. He refused. They asked where he kept the original. He said, 'Abroad.' He objected to being tried by all the members of the Aziza SMT, who overruled his objection. On July 29, 1995 he was charged with faxing the text of Bello-Fadile's defence in an attempt to enable the colonel escape punishment. He was also charged with faxing a letter written by Shehu Sani*. In his judgement, Aziza said that faxing the two documents abroad amounted to a signal for Britain and America to invade Nigeria in support of the alleged coup plotters!

Ransome-Kuti still regards the tribunal and its judgement with deep contempt. 'They were so stupid as to think that I could do that'.*

It was not the first time Ransome-Kuti would be accused of plotting to overthrow a government. A Gwagwalada Magistrate Court accused him of plotting to overthrow Babangida in 1992. Fawehinmi, Falana, Baba Omojola and Olusegun Maiyegun were charged with him on June 15, 1992. Before they were charged, Clement Akpamgbo, the Attorney General of the Federation and Minister of Justice, had said that 'certain groups of individuals who paraded themselves as human rights activists and democratic campaigners' had planned to overthrow the Federal Government. He said the government had stumbled on a 'secret plan to illegally engineer a change' of government. After their arrest, Ransome-Kuti and the other activists had been driven to the Lagos State Police Command, Ikeja, where they were asked to sign a document saying that if they stopped campaigning against the government they would be pardoned. They refused to do that. Therefore, they were detained in Kuje Prison and subsequently charged with treason. Because he had suffered so much in detention, he slumped in the court. Alarmed, Fela, his musician brother, went to Gwagwalada to lay a siege in the court premises.

On one occasion, at the Security Group, he was caught for trying to smuggle out messages. Instead of stopping, he quickly devised other effective means of violating their rule in order to

---

* The letter informed Dr. Ransome-Kuti of the nature of his trial before the tribunal.

* Commander L.M.O. Fabiyi, Rebecca Onyabi Ikpe and Moses Ayegba were also jailed because of Bello-Fadile's defense. Benson Ikepe and Anthony Awoniyi were declared wanted for the same reason.

survive. One of these was sewing messages to the hem of his trousers, which he was sending home to be laundered. Where did he get the needle and the thread? He said, 'From somewhere.'

I read his copy of Nelson Mandela's *Long* Walk *to Freedom**. He agreed with me that the book is a document of inspiration. We both thought that anyone interested in personal courage, self sacrifice and the spirit of collective diligence should read that book. On page 238 of the hardcover edition, Mandela writes: 'Our case was far more than a trial of legal issues between the crown and a group of people charged with breaking the law. It was a trial of strength, a test of the power of a moral idea versus an immoral one.' Ransome-Kuti and I felt that Mandela was meditating on our case.

Again, on page 601, this moving tribute: 'In Plato's allegory of the metals, the philosopher classifies men into groups of gold, silver and lead. Oliver Tambo was pure gold; there was gold in his intellectual brilliance, gold in his warmth and humanity, gold in his tolerance and generosity, gold in his unfailing loyalty and self sacrifice. As much as I respected him as a leader, that is how much I loved him as a man.'

'Mandela', I told Ransome-Kuti, when I finished reading that passage, 'is not just paying a deserving tribute to the dead freedom fighter; he is also trying to humanise the rest of us'.

That day a soldier brought to our cell a copy of *TELL* magazine which had the picture of Osa Director, one of its journalists, in chains. He had written a story on the Petroleum Trust Fund, which the government considered inciting. He spent 36 days in detention, many of those days he spent in chains. We felt sad for a country, which was grovelling under a dictator's jackboot.

---

* Nelson Mandela, *Long Walk to Freedom*. (New York: Little Brown and Company, 1994.)

In the second week of September 1995, May Ellen Mofe-Damijo visited the Security Group. The meeting was held ostensibly for Olu to plead Mrs Mofe-Damijo's case. He wanted us to know that, contrary to what we might have heard, she had not handed over her editor, Charles-Obi to the Intelligence. I was angry that May Ellen, who was a professional friend, allowed herself to be used by the security, but it was Ransome-Kuti who expressed the anger: 'I don't think that this is the right place to discuss what the publisher of *Classique* has done to her editor. As a publisher, she should know that she did not do the right thing'.

We found solace in Christianity and Islam as we waited for Abacha to decide our fate. After three weeks of persistent request by Rebecca Ikpe and Lieutenant-Colonel T.O. Miri-Dashe, I started attending the Christian service on Sundays. The service, for me, was more of a secular ceremony than a religious one.

On one of those Sundays, Lieutenant-Colonel Izourgu, who was the pastor of the congregation said, 'Our Bible reading today is taken from the first letter of Apostle Paul to the Corinthians: Chapter 13 verses 1-13,. I read the passage on Love:

> 'I may be able to speak the languages of human beings and even of angels, but if I have no love, my speech is no more than a noisy gong or a clanging bell. I may have the gift of inspired preaching; I may have all knowledge and understand all secrets; I may have all the faith needed to move mountains— but if I have no love, I am nothing. I may give away everything I have, and even give up my body to be burnt— but if I have no love, this does me no good. Love is patient and kind; it is not jealous or conceited or

> proud; love is not ill mannered or selfish or irritable;
> love does not keep a record of wrongs; love is not
> happy with evil, but is happy with the truth. Love
> never gives up; and its faith, hope and patience never
> fail...'

It goes on to say that love is eternal, that when everything passes away only three things will remain: faith, hope and love, 'and the greatest of these is love'.

How I enjoyed reading that passage and the interpretations that followed in those days of hate. Of course, Paul, the most literate of the authors of New Testament epistles, is not talking of carnal love; he is interested in spiritual love, an aspect of which Prophet Muhammad describes in *Hadith* as *uhibul watani*—the love of one's country, which he recommends as an important obligation. I enjoyed much more many of the moving choruses we sang. My favourite, which would later become my refrain in Makurdi Prison, is:

> *Abraham's blessings are mine*
> *Abraham's blessings are mine*
> *I'm blessed in the morning*
> *I'm blessed in the evening*
> *Abraham's blessings are mine*

With D.A.D. Usman leading, the muslim congregation also read the potent *Ya Sin* many times to *fortify* all of us.

At the Sunday devotion, which followed the puerile October broadcast by Abacha, Anyanwu was asked to pray. Crushed by grief, just like many of us, she challenged God: *where are you God? For how long are we going to wait? You say ask and you shall be given. We have asked many times but we have not been given. We pray day and night yet we are still in here. Why do you refuse to listen to us? Have you for-*

saken us? We have prayed and prayed and we are tired of praying. We are still asking you to beat with merciless blows those who are treating us like this. We are asking you to snatch this country from the evil men and kick them... She went on and on, enervated by a crisis of faith, which many believers suffer each time they feel abandoned by their gods. Anyanwu was not happy that the Security Group would not allow her to sign and send cheques home. She felt betrayed by some highly placed individuals who would not come to her aid. Obviously, she could not bear the pains of the stories of her relationships with men, which were making the rounds. She worried so much about the dwindling fortunes of her magazine. She caught herself sobbing several times in detention for other intensely personal reasons.

In the morning of October 1, 1995, after a long vigil, armed officers of the DMI descended in two trucks and a jeep. They looked set to commit murder. *Has Abacha decided to execute the officers already condemned to death?*

The day before, our cells had been searched. Two transistor radio sets were seized. We were left in no doubt that things were not at ease. But thanks to the immense pressure mounted on Abacha in form of pleas for clemency, he did not announce that anyone had been executed, *a few* hours ago, as Bali said when Vatsa and others were executed by Babangida. For us, that in itself was a kind of victory; it was a victory over death. 'In consideration of the earnest pleas of our friends and in the spirit of national reconciliation which has been the centre-piece of this administration's policy,' Abacha dragged on his lines as if he was not happy, 'government has decided to commute the sentences on the coup plotters. This situation will be reviewed at the appropriate time.' My sentence was reduced to fifteen years after the broadcast.

He also made it known in his speech that he would leave office in 1998, *if the transition programme worked out smoothly*. That was a big if. If there were civilians deceived by the 1998 dateline, military officers who knew Abacha were not. Abacha, they said, had a history of sitting tight in office. They said that when he was shuffled as Chief of Army Staff to Chief of Defence Staff, he refused to vacate the 8th floor office in the Ministry of Defence Headquarters, Tafawa Balewa Square, for the new Chief of Army Staff. He also refused to leave the Flag-staff House, the traditional residence of Chief of Army Staff on the 2nd Avenue, Ikoyi. Even when he moved to Abuja as Head of State, the Flagstaff House was still retained as if it was his private property. He changed it to Defence House.

That night the Nigerian Television Authority (NTA) showed a 50-minute documentary titled *Special Programme on the 1995 Coup Plot Attempt*. The narrator said the coup plotters planned to assassinate Abacha on 1 March at the Sallah pray-ing ground; they planned to storm the Presidential Villa; they planned to arrest all the GOCs; they planned to eliminate all officers from the rank of Brigadiers and above; and they planned to use senior retired officers for the operation, after which they would lay them off. It was all lies.

The narrator also said that when Bello-Fadile contacted Yar'Adua on the coup at Nicon-Noga Hilton Hotel, Abuja, he promised to support the coupists, but Obasanjo was not so receptive to the plan when he was briefed. The narrator said Ransome-Kuti had *illegally* obtained sensitive documents on the coup trial and faxed them to foreign countries. He said that Anyanwu was enlisted by Sanusi Mato to publish favourable articles that would save Gwadabe, her friend and a shareholder in her company. The documentary played up the involvement of Akinyemi in a plot to overthrow Abacha because it looked credible. All lies!

As soon as he learnt about this propaganda, Obasanjo sent out letters to some of his friends, family members, aids and Papa Ajasin, a leading opposition politician, to assure them that he and other convicts were innocent. His letter to Ajasin read in part:

> '*Sir, there is need to intensify efforts in three or four directions—Release of M.K.O. Abiola, release of the so-called coup plotters, rejection of a three year transition programme. It is another deceit. If the brief period when he came extends to five years, three years will extend to six years or more unless he is given a chase through rejection and a drastic reduction and an arrangement that incorporates solution of June 12. All like-minded forces must work in the three areas together and at once. None should be allowed to slip. I believe that the intrepid press and the international community will not let off… If any of these issues is allowed to recede to the background or sidetracked, it will be forgotten. I hope and pray that the resolution of these four issues be one of the legacies that you will leave behind…' ***

Obasanjo, who had said that Abiola was not the messiah Nigeria needed, had become a strong supporter of the struggle for *June 12*. Perhaps if he had initially supported the campaign to de-annul the results, if he had not been part of the ING, we would not be heading to prison.

It was gratifying that all the reports in the papers and magazines, which were smuggled into our cells, doubted or re-

---

* *TEMPO*, 26 October, 1995.

jected outrightly the veracity of the government version of the coup story. October had come without bringing garlands of liberty, but intimations that we would soon be sent to jail. We had waited so long.

On October 14, 1995, we were hauled in the *Black Maria* and dumped in Maximum Security Prison, Kirikiri. For the first time, all the so-called coup plotters were in the same place. It was ludicrous that, although we had all been convicted for the same crime, that was the first time many of us met.

We were distributed to various prisons on one-convict-per-prison basis.

EIGHT

~~~~~~~~

Pushed into
the Limbo

Wednesday October 18, 1995. A warder, who was reeking of *burukutu*,* came to my dingy cell at the crack of dawn and ordered me to pack. Manacled and chained, I was not allowed to take my bath in the open air as we were forced to do in the last three days. There was no time to brush my teeth.

The *Black Maria* was waiting.

I shouted farewell to many of the prisoners on the death row with whom we had shared this block. When we got to the main gate, I saw a gathering of harried alleged coup plotters. It was abundantly clear that it was the season of our dispersal to different prisons in the country. A smooth transition from dark to darkness.

The warder led me to the Records where I collected my

---

* A locally brewed alcoholic beverage.

small sack of books and a medium size plastic bucket. When my two attempts at mounting the *Black Maria* failed because of the leg chains, an army Sergeant smartly pressed forward and hoisted my entire slender frame into the lorry. I sat between Lieutenant-Colonel R.D. Obiki and Anyanwu.

As we got to the Air Force base in Ikeja, the lorry screeched to a halt. Obasanjo, Obiki, Lieutenant-Colonel M.A. Igwe, Anyanwu, Matthew Popoola, Mbah, Major D.O. Obalisa, Lieutenant A. Olowookere and myself were all marched into a Charlie 130. Five fully armed infantry soldiers and eight warders and a wardress joined the plane for maximum security. As the plane surged through the clouds, its motion bestowed sobriety on us.

I looked at Obasanjo, who opened the Bible on his lap. Where did he get the inner strength to read? This was a former Head of State, innocent of the crime of treason, but now being treated as a common criminal. The only concession to his former status was that he was not in chains like the rest of us. I wanted to know how his mind was working, but because I was not sitting next to him, there was no way of finding out. What would the families of those who were killed for coup plotting during his regime think now? *That it serves him right?* Even though there was a difference between our 'treason' and that of the 1976 coupists, I imagined the aggrieved families of J. D. Gomwalk and the rest would not see it that way. Unlike General Yakubu Gowon, a deposed former Head of State, who stayed back in UK when he was accused of conspiring to assassinate General Murtala Muhammed, Obasanjo came back home from Copenhagen to face his accusers. I knew that even after the verdict of the tribunal, Obasanjo was still very much in the dark about the details of how he was framed. For more than three weeks, he was kept incommunicado in a cell at the Interrogation Centre where he was honoured with a dirty small mattress and a plastic plate.

Anyanwu, the only woman victim in the plane, also caught my attention. She drank some water straight from a plastic bottle. *Was it to calm down her nerves? What would happen to her business now, where she made herself the centre? How would she cope in jail?* It seemed to me that her professional ambition in print journalism was to beat the impressive records of Dr. Doyin Abiola, Bilikisu Yusuf, Agbeke Ogunsanwo, May Ellen Mofe-Damijo and Ama Ogan. Anyanwu deserved encouragement, not this kind of bashing. I wished I had the power to set her free.   ‘

At 11:00 AM, we had our first stopover at the Air Force base in Makurdi. Obiki and I were dropped off. Lieutenant-Colonel P.B.O. Akhigbe, the Commanding Officer of 72 Paratroops Battalion, led the convoy that received us. You would think the convoy had come for the most dangerous criminals: 2 Steyr trucks full of armed soldiers, 2 station wagon cars and 2 pick-up vans with armed policemen and the SSS men. The siren began to wail as we disembarked from the C130. The deafening noise and our fearsome presence woke up the sleepy capital of Benue State as we passed through the elite area known as GRA* to the heart of the city itself.

The moment our convoy turned towards Makurdi Prison, in Wadata, a throng of onlookers poured into its precincts to see the *important* criminals. The crowd looked like excited flies feeding on open wounds. When the main gate of this tomb was shut behind us, I felt my heart sink. I stood lost.

It was strange to me that the well-fed and well-armed soldiers, who believed that security was all about grand drama, handed us over to some hungry looking, seemingly helpless

---

‘ Government Reservation Area

warders whose only weapons were walls, bars, locks, chains, and batons.

We were searched thoroughly, stripped of our clothes. They removed our shoes. They yanked off our wristwatches. They took my sack of books from me and flung it into a small room full of cobwebs. Because we were now 'prisoners', they brought two pairs of prison uniforms very quickly. A pair of shorts, and an undersized shirt for me. One similar pair also for Obiki, who would soon be taken to Gboko Prison. We were then marched to the office of Chief Superintendent of Prisons (CSP), Iorbee Ihagh. Short, dark in complexion, this officer would soon demonstrate in many ways that he was one of the civil servants who crossed over to the prison system not to make the institution a reformative place that it ought to be but a hellhole.

As the custom demanded, we had to tell him why we had been sent to prison. When Obiki finished, Ihagh said, 'I am surprised at you, Colonel. An officer of your rank should have known better. If I were you, I would have reported Akinyemi immediately. You see, if you had done that you won't be in prison now, you would be somewhere else enjoying yourself.'

His telephone rang. After a rather long conversation, he said 'No. Don't come now. I am very busy, addressing the new convicts who have been brought from Lagos. Yes, the coup plotters. It's a lot of work. They gave me two of them. You see, Yes. They know I have been doing a good job. You see.'

When he finally hung up, I, too, told him the story of my arrest and trial before a kangaroo court. His response was vapid, 'You see, I studied in the US. That's why they call me Americana here. I know everything about America; I know how journalists work in the US. You see, no journalists in the US would dabble into a military affair the way you've done. What's your business with the military?' I thought at that first encounter that

Ihagh was dishonest. I would soon have concrete evidence.

The telephone rang again.

This call must have been from his boss, for he quickly recited the lock-up number as he sat stiff on his chair, 'All correct, sir!'

He told his two assistants, John and Amaye, that the Comptroller would be coming to see us the following day. He then said, 'Well, convicts: your warrants say you would be in prison till July 13, 2010. As you know, there is no remission for court-martial convicts. I can assure you that you are in good hands.'

I thought his emphasis on *July 13, 2010* was a very unkind cut.

He pressed his table bell and waited. He pressed it again, harder. His orderly who rushed in was ordered to take us to the yard.

As we entered the enclosure called the yard, everywhere was quiet. All the prisoners had been locked up. Only the curious ones broke the temporary ban imposed on them and peeped through their windows to see the coup plotters. Warders stood in some strategic locations. I heard one of them say, *'Na dem be this?'* as we stepped into the dilapidated gate that led to the yard. We were escorted to the office of Baba Igbira, the *kolanut*-chewing old man who was the Keeper and asked to sit on the floor as he addressed us:

'Una welcome o. Welcome. Na Black Maria dem take bring you come or plane? Make you just dey thank God. Thank God well, well. We don hear about una case for radio. You just dey lucky. Na God save una o. You for don die. If no be say Abacha dey kind e for don kill una o. Your offence na big offence. Which place better pass: prison or grave? So make you just dey thank God. One day go be one day when we go tell you say your paper don come. We go open that big gate gbraaam, and say, tefi; make you

comot. Na to go be that o. Make you no worry. Warderman no be police. E no be soldier. E be human being. If you respect am, you go enjoy am. Na him be your master now o. No prisoner is important. Thank you. Thank you so much.'

He replaced his headgear and asked one of his staff to take me to A3, a small cell located between two armed robbery suspects cells. The seven-by-four cell was bed-bug infested and lice-laden. Its walls were murky. I was allowed to clean up its gritty, slimy and dirty floor before my first intolerable cold night. There was a small corner that I used as my bathroom and toilet. I knew the roof would leak during raining seasons because of the holes in the corrugated iron sheets. The armed robbers who were the last occupants of the cell before me were publicly executed in Makurdi in April, 1995. They scribbled their names on the walls before they were taken away. This would turn out to be the place where I spent all my term in this prison.

In the morning, we were led to Ihagh's office.

'Squat down! Squat down! Squat down!'

We obeyed them and fell into the frozen silence of conquered warriors. When I looked up, the photographs of Abacha, the head of the ruling junta, Wing Commander Joshua Obademi, the Military Administrator of Benue State, and Alhaji Garba Gora Baidu, the then Comptroller-General of the Nigeria Prisons Service, stared down balefully at us. Mrs. Joy Oka Aghi, the acting Comptroller of prisons in Benue State, cleared her throat and said,

'Are you with us, Mr. Ajibade?'

Yes, I said. A lie. My mind was somewhere else. I was thinking that here was another proof that we were still living in a savage age. I was also telling myself that Franz Kafka would like this scene so much. In novel after novel, Kafka demonstrates how absurd situations could transform human beings into grotesque figures. Is it not so appropriate that he uses the law and the penal system as his constant *leitmotifs* to depict a nightmare world in which humankind sometimes find itself?

'You are welcome, then,' Aghi continued.

'Welcome to this prison. It is not our duty to question what has brought you here. We are not allowed to do that because we are civil servants. You are not here for punishment. You are here as punishment. My advice to you is that you should comport yourselves. The warrant that brought you here, if this paper could be called a warrant, says you should be kept incommunicado until further notice. But that does not mean we shall impede your movement within the yard. As long as you obey the rules of this prison, I don't think you will have any problem. You are in good hands. Do you have anything to say?'

I asked, 'Do we have any right at all as political prisoners?'

'Of course, you have. Or you should have. But I would have to clear that with the highest authorities. Any other question?'

She looked in the direction of Obiki, who said nothing. His own puritan Christian faith seemed to have imbued him with the stamina of a doormat. He stayed uncomplaining till he was moved to Gboko Prison on November 30, 1995.

'Stand still everywhere!'

All the warders drew themselves still and saluted. Mrs. Aghi had finished her assignment. She didn't bother to return the compliment. Stone-faced, she walked past us stiffly, quickly and grimly. We were dismissed.

Back in the cell, Ukidi, a senior warder gave me an old blanket, which I was supposed to spread on the damp floor. There was no bed. But a couple of hours later he came to speak to me through the barb wired window:

'I don dey look for mattress since. I no want make you just dey sleep for floor like that. E no good at all. Thank God: I don find one mattress now. But you go find me something. Ground no level. E no level at all.'

I feigned ignorance. So, he sent an interpreter at once. But where would I get the money? He said he would wait until I was allowed to keep some money. The mattress that he sold to me was tattered and begrimed with age. He also sent an enamel plate and a cup. My stomach turned.

The evil of Abacha permitted no witness. Which was why the prison was asked to keep us in solitary confinement. No one could visit us. No communication with the outside world. Only special warders should guard us. Forgetting that truth would prevail, the regime of Abacha did not want the truth of our case to be shared with anyone.

My pregnant wife did not know of this directive. So, on November 4, 1995 she travelled all the way from Ibadan, a distance of about 1,800 kilometres, to visit me.* She was turned back at the gate. Bunmi went straight to the house of the Comptroller of Prisons in Benue State and told her she would not go home until she saw me. Mrs. Aghi pleaded that the only concession she could make was to allow Mayowa, our two-year-old son, who had been asking his mother for my whereabouts, to see me. When Mayowa was eventually brought to meet me for less than five minutes, the boy could not recognise me. Apart from my thick beard, which I wasn't wearing at home, pimples had already taken complete possession of my face. At that emotion-laden meeting, I said to Ihagh,

'See the crazy thing you people are doing to me. What kind

---

* Tunji Wusu, a member of our staff, accompanied her on the trip.

f violence is this? If I have wronged Abacha, has my family
lso offended him? What has this boy done to him to deserve
his kind of pain? What has my pregnant wife done to deserve
his punishment?'

Ihagh was a bit sober when he said, 'Don't take this out on
he. We are just errand boys. '

He hit the bull's-eye. They too knew that they were incapa-
le of reforming criminals. The majority of them ceased to no-
ce the rot of the place because they were part of the decay.
hey were the real prisoners without chains.

Nov_ember 10, 1995, the news frittered through the walls
that in Port Harcourt Prison, Ken Saro-Wiwa and eight of
is Ogoni compatriots had been hanged. The Ogoni Civil Dis-
urbances Special Tribunal headed by Justice Ibrahim Ndali
uta had convicted them after a grossly unfair and politically
hotivated trial. As soon as he realised that the tribunal had be-
ome a kangaroo court, Saro-Wiwa asked his lawyers, among
hom were some of the most prominent defenders of the op-
ressed in our country: Fawehinmi, Olisa Agbakoba, and Falana,
 withdraw from the case so that they would not give that tri-
unal the dignity it did not deserve. He told them that he would
rove his innocence in his allocutus. After his conviction, many
eople asked: *How far will Abacha go with the Ogoni is-*
ue? Will he allow reason to prevail? No, he did not. He
ent to the end of the line itself. He hanged the activists of the
Movement for the Survival of the Ogoni People (MOSOP) and
cid was allegedly poured on their remains. At that time, the
Commonwealth Prime Ministers Conference was taking place
 Auckland.

The main charge against Saro-Wiwa by Joseph Daudu, the
rosecutor, was that he threatened to deal with the vultures,

which the tribunal accepted was an indirect reference to four prominent moderate Ogoni men, who were set ablaze in Giokoo, where Saro-Wiwa was allegedly slated to address a rally.

Yet, Saro-Wiwa, the President of MOSOP, whom I knew, was a man of peace. He loved good arguments. The passion with which he made his points was a passion that appealed to many lovers and seekers of truth, justice and fairplay. His vision made his people see clearly the starkness of their miseries. He provided the lead, which he expected the Niger-Delta people to follow.

I felt diminished by the execution of Ken and the other compatriots. Downcast, I lost appetite for my miserable food. Then anger and bitterness took over. On August 2, 1995, he had smuggled out a letter to the General Secretary of the Association of Nigerian Authors, Dr. Wale Okediran, reporting that he was in good health, that he was hopeful of the best but prepared for the worst. He wrote that he had been much comforted by the support he had got from writers in Nigeria and abroad. He also said that he felt sad about my arrest and trial. He probably thought that we would meet again. That we were being ruled by a bunch of murderers was sad enough. It was sadder still that the United Nations (UN) and the Commonwealth waited for Abacha to snuff the lives of the Ogoni nationalists before they began to do a mop-up operation.

The only picture of Saro-Wiwa frozen in my mind was that short writer who came to our office for the last time in May 1993 sucking at an unlit pipe. He had come for our roundtable in simple *adire* and a pair of trousers. As he lit his pipe, he told us that he was not trying to take the Niger-Delta out of Nigeria. He said he would prefer to remain in Nigeria so long as there was social justice. After the interview, he suggested that we should condemn the new decree, *Treason and Treasonable*

Offences Decree No 29 of 1993, which Babangida just minted. He argued that the regime intended to trap him with the decree. However, we did not condemn that decree in our write-up on him. Ironically, two years later, I was sent to jail based on the decree, or a variant of it.

As a friend, I bear testimony to his total commitment to the Ogoni struggle. Indeed, in November 1992 in London, he had asked Adewale Maja-Pearce of *Index On Censorship* to persuade me to take up the editorship of a quarterly he was preparing to float. I told Maja-Pearce, that we would soon start something of our own and that I would not work for a propagandist. I believed that description of him was right until a couple of months later when he took the late poet Sesan Ajayi and I to the death-field that was his homeland.

The shocking realities on the ground indicated to me that I had judged him unfairly. The result of oil exploration in Ogoni since 1958: oil spillage which had ravaged the soil, polluted the water and made the air thick with dust; gas flares, pipelines, flow stations and oilfields had taken over the Ogoni farmlands. In response to this injustice, the Ogoni embarked on a nonviolent way to ask the government of Nigeria for adequate compensation. In a pamphlet titled *Ogoni Bill Of Rights*, it is stated succinctly that it is not fair that the Ogoni who produce $30 billion worth of crude oil should live in abject poverty.

But in a dark alliance with the oil companies, Abacha set up the Internal Security Task Force, a military squad headed by Lieutenant-Colonel Paul Okuntimo, to quell the burning outrage of the Ogoni. The killing of the outspoken Ogoni nationalists was the ultimate attempt to silence their people. *Why is the ghost of this martyred intellectual still stalking our terrain most valiantly?* The reason is simple: the unfair treatment of the oil-bearing areas, which he raised his voice against, has not stopped. The corpses of the Ogoni 9 may have been burnt to ashes, I know they live in the minds of a lot of their people who are inspired and emboldened by their courage.

January 1, 1996. I got a newspaper cutting with the following statement made by Obasa: *'The office of the magazine division of the Independent Communications Network Limited, publishers of TheNEWS, TEMPO and TEMPO FOOTBALL magazines, was this morning, Sunday 31 December, 1995, torched by arsonists who escaped after setting fire that destroyed property worth millions of naira. The office located on the first floor of Tejumola House, along the new Isheri Road, of Ikeja, Lagos, houses the newsroom and production centre of the three magazines. It is the only floor of the four-storey building that was burnt. The timely intervention of the men of the fire service department who were alerted by neighbours prevented the fire from spreading to other floors of the building. The management of this organisation has reported the case to the police. We believe the arsonists wanted to take advantage of the New Year holiday to enact this tragedy knowing full well that human traffic in the office and the neighbourhood would be very low. We also believe it could not have been an accident resulting from electricity faults because the power supply to the building has been cut off by the National Electric Power Authority (NEPA) for about three months now following an inconclusive agreement between the property owners and NEPA. Indeed we have had to run our operations with a private generating set which had been switched off since Friday 29 December 1995. We also rule out the possibility of a cover-up of theft because while extensive damage was caused by the fire, nothing was apparently olen. The police have arrested two security guards who re now helping their investigation'.*

What a way to start a New Year! In prison!

Makurdi Prison stank. It stank of rotten flesh, of excrement, of rat urine. It stank of many mouths unbrushed for 1any days. It stank of corruption as well. Could this be why so 1any prisoners and warders spat phlegm copiously here? Many f the warders were heavy drinkers of *burukutu*. Before he /as sacked, a warder would stagger to the yard everyday dead runk. Cigarette and *oturu* (local tobacco) had conquered some f them. Some of them smoked Indian hemp regularly. At the ack of my cell was an open cesspool. Each morning, around :00 AM, you would hear a shout of Lagos! Lagos! Lagos! ·om all corners of the prison. It was time for the inmates to arry the load of excrement from their cells to the dumping round, River Benue. The name for this exercise was *Running agos*. The smell in the air would be so thick and foul. Shouts f Wwata! Wwata! Wwata! filled the air thirty minutes later. he water gang would go to the same River Benue to fetch water or use in the kitchen. I had to make special arrangements to get ipe-borne water.

On May 11, 1997, when the Comptroller of Prisons, Albert a'ad, visited the prison and saw the water, he called the grey-aired man who was the most senior of the warders around and sked,

'Can you drink this yourself? Can you? Get me a cup there. 'ou have to drink this water. Drink it now. I say drink it.'

The old man, shaking and swaying like a tree in a storm, said :ammering,

'I-I-I c-an-n-ot ddrrriiinnk iiitt, ss-iier'.

'Are you refusing my order?'

'Nno, sirr. I-I no fit ddrriinkk am'.

'You think the inmates are not human beings like you?'

The fuming Sa'ad asked the old man to see him in his office the following day. Some of the warders said the Comptroller should have expended his energy on repairing the prison's long-neglected borehole.

Whenever one of his bosses was visiting from the headquarters, Ihagh would send for a cheap disinfectant, which the warders would sprinkle over the yard. Makurdi Prison looked like the worst of shanties. A compact abnormality walled round. A dark void menacingly enclosed with tall concrete walls. Built in the 1930s for labour conscripts by the British colonialists, it was one of the three prisons in Benue State. With one in Gboko and another in Otukpo. The smallest of these was Makurdi Prison, where the Tivs and the Idomas were engaged in a cut-throat rivalry. In the ranking of prisons, it fell in the category of a lock-up.

When I was there, more than half of the inmates were armed robbery suspects awaiting trial. There were petty thieves and rapists. There were two madmen. Some of the prisoners were products of broken homes. Some were children of frustrated soldiers arbitrarily laid off. Two were children of warders. Some were children of prostitutes. Just a few were kleptomaniacs who were caught several times still stealing in jail. Each time I had a word with them, they would tell several versions of their single stories and would come out of them chivalrous. At such times, the warders were the worst skeptics. Experience had taught them not to trust a prisoner. Trust carried no weight here.

For the habitual criminals, spending time in jail was part of the hazard of their own job. For those of them who did not have a place to lay their heads in the city or village, prison was a haven. The jailbirds kept coming back to this edge of abyss. When I read in *The Same River Twice* by Alice Walker that 'Death is easily preferred to imprisonment of any kind'*, I said: Oh, no! Not for these boys. Imprisonment was preferred to death. It was preferred to hunger on the streets. It was preferred to the burden of being regarded as outcasts. Like the palms of their hands, they knew so many prisons in Nigeria inside out. They talked glowingly of the ones they preferred. They spoke contemptuously of the ones they hated. For so many of the gang leaders, this prison was a fertile place of re-cruitment. It was also a training ground for new criminals.

As you listened to them sing hymns in tough, husky voices that pierced the walls, you would think the inmates were more religious than the Pope himself, until you heard them say at the end of their night prayers, 'God bless these *Barawo (*Thieves*)* '! Religion, for many of them, was sheer entertainment, just like their Saturday nights devoted to *swange**. It was not a cov-enant with God; it was a pact with mammon. Constantly, you would hear a prisoner say, *'I no know God o!'*

The graffiti I saw on one of the walls in the Maximum Secu-rity Prison, Kirikiri, 'CRY YOUR OWN CRY', had meaning here. There was no kindness in this place. Its inmates regarded Makurdi Prison as Alabama City. In this city, the *Sarki* or the Provost of the prisoners had to be a tyrant. He must be very wicked. Schooled in prison wisdom, he knew that his position was just a means of survival. If the authority wanted him to report on warders, he would gladly do so. If the warders wanted him to implicate his fellow prisoners, he would do so.

Each of the cells also had its own Provost, Chief Judge, Ad-

---

* Alice Walker, *The Same River Twice* (New York: Pocket Books, 1996).

* The Tiv traditional dances and songs

viser, Inspector- General of Police, Deputy Inspector-General of Police, Commissioners and Cleaners. Because they had been to court many times, they knew how to conduct mock court sessions. They knew how to imitate all the judges in the Benue State Judiciary.Their court scenes would look real but for the harsh and arbitrary judgements of the judges all the time. After the judgements the entire cell would raise a loud chorus: AS THE COURT PLEASES! The most humiliating of the sentences was serving time in the gas chamber. Which meant sleeping near the shit bucket for a month or two. The judges sometimes, mostly during the searing heat, would ask an erring inmate to fan the provost from dusk to dawn for two weeks. This way, Alabama City devoured itself.

But the Keeper's punishment of the Indian Hemp smokers was always a special spectacle. The offenders would be stripped naked. Then the Keeper would say, 'Gif dem twelve'. That meant that each of the offenders should be given twelve strokes of the cane. Then the lashes of whip would crash on the naked flesh. The warders always knew instinctively that the offenders' tears were not genuine. Whipping in this place was preferred to 'batoning'. For the baton was used to break bones.

'A faceless group which called itself Committed Patriots flooded Lagos and other cities with posters carrying the following inscription: *To anarchist, Professor Wole Soyinka and his NALICON cohorts, to NADECO chiefs and their sponsors, we say: he who sows the wind shall reap the whirl-wind, you may run but you can't hide. Take this as bulletin number one.* That's not all. You must have heard that Abacha had labelled Soyinka in *The Washington Times* as a terrorist. Chief Tom Ikimi, his Minister for Foreign Affairs, Dr. Walter

Ofonagoro, Minister for Information, and Alhaji Wada Nas, his Minister for Special Duties, denigrate Soyinka's person. His house in Abeokuta has been vandalised. But Soyinka's civic conscience is stronger.' This was the reply to one of the notes I sent to a friend in 1996.

Subsequent updates indicated that Soyinka used his international fame and immense talent to sensitise the world to Abacha's bestiality. The short wave station, Radio Democratic International (now renamed Radio Kudirat) was a very effective mobilisation tool. He ran the radio with other patriots among whom were Dr. Kayode Fayemi, Dr. Olaokun Soyinka, Gbolahan Olalemi, Dayo Benson, George Noah, Makin Soyinka, Olawale Oshun, Yinka Johnson and Dele Olawale. 'I Knew it was a dangerous thing to undertake', said Olalemi, one of the members of the techincal crew. 'But I wanted a society that would be just and equitable.'* Those who presented passionate programmes on that underground radio, which became a fearless voice of the opposition abroad included Chief Anthony Enahoro, Professors Sola Adeyeye, Julius Ihonvbere and Bolaji Akinyemi. General Alani Akinrinade, Senator Ahmed Bola Tinubu and several other people and organisations were very instrumental to the funding of Radio Kudirat.

Soyinka always rang true in his characterisation of Abacha as a psychopath. Then the tyrant pinned him as one of the brains behind the sporadic bombings in Nigeria. He was declared wanted for that imaginary treason. If he had not left the country in 1994, shortly after the SSS had seized his international passport, he would have ended up in jail again. Given his record as that man, in those days of barefaced robbery of the people's

---

* Olalemi was very much involved in the running of *Radio Freedom* in Lagos. He was able to move the entire equipment from place to place without being detected. He was later arrested by the DMI, not because of this underground radio but because of his association with Olorunyomi.

democratic rights, who stormed a radio station with a loaded gun, only to play a recorded tape that was critical of Akintola, the then Premier of Western Region; given his record as that writer who did not only condemn the Nigerian civil war but went to the war-front in Biafra to sell the idea of a third force to some of its bright officers; given his record as that professor who, in 1983, chased some of the scoundrels of the NPN out of the University of Ife; and given his record as the leader of the National Liberation Council of Nigeria (NALICON) whose motto was: *By all means necessary*, it was quite understandable that Abacha would be afraid of him. In a long and very enviable career spanning writing (in all genres) and human rights activism, Soyinka has demonstrated, at great risks to his own life, that acquiescence in the face of military dictatorship, or civilian tyranny, is a symptom of a deadly disease in the soul. As a veteran of the struggle for democratic ideals, this radiant humanist marched through many dangerous paths and came out of them triumphant.

There was big a bang on the floor in A2 cell, the most crowded of the cells for armed robbery suspects. One of the inmates sprang to attention and saluted the provost of the cell. He asked for permission to introduce the new prisoner.

'Carry on', the provost commanded from his imperial corner.

'A new comer from Alabama Country now in Alabama City searching for *garri*, *kunu*, *gabza*, *degedege*, *kwarakata*, mosquitoes, bedbugs and *oturu*. Permission to treat him *baaad*!'

The whole cell was quiet while it waited for the decision of the provost, who cleared his throat and, because he was in a good mood, pleaded, *'Treat am gentle.'*

The Inspector General of the cell then raised his voice as he delivered the Grand Rule:

'Abacha is the Head of State of Alabama Country. He is an idiot. He is a nonentity. He is a criminal. He is a robber. He is greedy. Nobody knows him in this Alabama City. The only president, the only Head of State, the only governor, in this great city where there is order, is the provost. Now: bend down, hold your ears and greet him like this: Good evening, *sarki*. Good evening, *sarki*. Good evening, *sarki*.'

The new inmate, shouting, obeyed. He was marched to all the officials of the cell to pay them respect. The rest of the members of the cell he greeted thus,

'Good evening, cell members. I want to go.'

The cell members chorused, 'No way!'

The provost who was the high priest of the initiation ceremony then asked the cell,

'He weigh? He weigh?'

They all chorused, *'He weigh!'*

'Now, sing three new popular songs of Alabama Country.' Another officer made a request.

The voice of the new man was golden. The cell enjoyed his songs. Members clapped and danced.

But the initiation was not over. The Inspector-General moved to the centre of the cell holding what they called Penal Code, which no official could touch without his permission.

'Silence in the cell. I now read the sacred Penal Code. Every offence under Section A carries 21 days in gas chamber: fighting, stealing, homosexuality, coup attempt, smoking of indian hemp, insulting a cell officer, habitual coming to prison and urinating on the cell floor. Every offence under Section B carries 14 days in gas chamber: refusing lawful orders, interfering in official matters, dusting of blanket or clothes in the cell, contempt of court, talking when the cell is locked and nakedness in the cell. Every offence under Section C carries any punishment: pouring water on the cell floor, making noise at late hours, blocking the air conditioners (windows) and combing in the cell.'

The new comer said he would obey the Penal Code of Alabama City. The provost who sat like a king then said, 'Welcome to Alabama City.' And he started smoking *oturu* as he sang a popular love song in Tiv. A warder passed by. He greeted him. They both laughed as he said, *'We dey enjoy, Oga. Nothing spoil. Only women we no get.'* Another inmate then rendered a flawless performance of *Is this Love* by Bob Marley. Desolate night finally came.

T omidel, one of the convicts in the back cells, raised an alarm sometime in May 1996.
'Warder! Warder!'
I thought another inmate had died.
'Warder! Warder!'
There was a stampede in the yard. I heard the door of the cell open as the warders brought out the alleged culprits.
'Na lie. I no do am. Na lie.' The culprits pleaded.
But Tomidel did not relent.
'My eye never see this kind thing before. Man dey f—k another man's yansh! Haba!
It was a case of sodomy. Since the warders did not catch them at it, the alleged offenders were not punished. But the authority decided to increase the potash (*kanwun*) in the prison food. They believed that it would kill the sexual urge of the prisoners. But the prison still throbbed with pent-up lust.

S ome prisoners who went out to fetch water at the River Benue came in chatting about the fall of Sultan Ibrahim Dasuki on Saturday April 20, 1996. They were too impatient to listen to the reasons given on the radio for his dethronement and banishment to Taraba. But later that night, I learnt from a warder that the government had said that he had brought disrepute to the institution of Emirship as an accused at the Failed Banks Tribunal and that he had desecrated Islam.*

'How'? I asked.

No detail.

Only that he disregarded constituted authority. Of course, that authority was Abacha, or his regime of absolute scum. I was told Sultan Muhammadu Maccido had replaced him. Maccido was the man chosen by the Kingmakers on November 6, 1988. But Babangida upturned the verdict of the people because Dasuki was his personal friend. He never bothered about the carnage in Sokoto that came in the wake of that blatant rigging.

The two hundred and fifty prisoners in this prison were so sunk in the mud of sorrow, they had no strength to shout for joy. No lasting friendship, no permanent enmity, only common interest. This common interest was food, which, apart from the daily routine of counting of inmates, was the only significant activity here, not just for the inmates, but also the warders whose salaries were never paid on time. The prison food, which they called *gabza*, was *garri* and corn flour. Rice and beans were very rare. The regular fish was measly. Beef donated by the Tor Tiv, Alfred Torkula, was only served during Christmas. They called the small kitchen the *Powerhouse* because it was the heart of survival on this bleak spot. Prisoners were not posted to the kitchen as cooks if they were not ready to pay the Keeper,

---

* Many failed bank executives were suffering in detention at this time.

the Yardmaster and his assistant. The Storekeeper, the Ration Clerk and the kitchen warders knew that they owed allegiance to the man in charge of the prison, not to the prisoners. They and the food contractors had to guarantee his own share of the food items everyday. The items not supplied would be on paper as 'regularly supplied'. Food contractors would bring chaff as grains and Ihagh would accept them. The kitchen was the reason why two cats came into the yard every night! They would move from cell to cell foraging for the prisoners' leftovers. It would seem that the kitchen was where many big rats in Wadata loved to hold their emergency meetings in the night. I should know because if you stayed in my cell, you would see almost everything that went on in the kitchen, the ration office and the little store.

I saw how some of the warders shared the palm-oil among themselves, how they shared the salt, how they shared maggi cubes, how they shared raw food and cooked food, how they shared peppers and onions meant for their inmates. I saw how some of them even made away with the prisoners' plates, cups, blankets and buckets. I witnessed how many of the warders and some of the wardresses were always happy to share the free meat whenever a cow died of a disease in the abattoir that was very close to the prison.

Yet in this prison, there was once a riot over food. According to two lifers, the food contractor brought corn flour, instead of rice, which the prisoners rejected. They chose that moment to vent their anger on the prison authority and the Nigerian justice system which kept many inmates waiting for trial for a long period of time. Warders on duty scaled the walls as they were chased. Several prisoners escaped before the mobile police were called in. For more than two hours the prisoners engaged the police with the prison-made weapons while the police sent a heavy dose of tear gas into the yard. The prisoners stopped fighting when they were threatened with live bullets. That was when a reinforced team of warders regained entry, fully armed with cutlasses, batons and other types of incongruous weapons. At the end of the riot, seven inmates were killed and so many were seriously injured. This was Sunday, February 19, 1989.

Indiscipline was rife among warders. The junior ranks argued fiercely with their seniors and most times disobeyed orders— a rare occurrence in the military locations where I had been detained.

Makurdi Prison* had no space for a mosque, church, recreation centre or workshop. The five blocks (E Block was the only modern addition) that made up this prison were crammed on a tiny strip of land very close to the River Benue. The two big trees in the yard were used as Purgatory where new inmates sat before they were admitted to their appropriate cells. This contraption was not a place to take a walk. There was a makeshift clinic, which was always starved of drugs until the Petroleum Trust Fund (PTF) started making drugs available in 1997. Before then, I witnessed many deaths of inmates from dysentery, malaria, tuberculosis, typhoid, small pox, epilepsy, syphilis, ulcer, diarrhoea and infections of urinary tracts. Whenever this happened, I felt unsafe.

They were so used to inmates dying here that death seemed to be a way of decongesting the prison. The dead would be wrapped in a blanket, or sometimes in black polythene bags. They would then be hauled to the burial ground at Ankpa's

---

* On account of the interviews given by Chief Bola Ige and I about the appalling conditions of the place after our release, the prison has now been moved to a better site.

quarters. With one hoe and two cutlasses, the inmates would bury them in shallow graves. Many of those who died had been awaiting trial for several years. The nurses could do little without drugs or equipment. What struck me most was the morbid transformation of human beings in this place. Sometimes they would bring fresh arrivals, those who had not been damaged by police brutality. Robust fellows with flesh on their cheeks and lively eyes. Two weeks later, many of them would dry up. This amazing disintegration always brought with it an acrid stench.

They let out the awaiting trial prisoners twice a week for what the warders called fresh air, as if such existed in the yard. Fearing that the prisoners would escape, the warders would order them to sit in one place. This was the time for the prisoners to de-louse their clothes and blankets. There were cases of inmates who ran mad in the cells. To observe whether the cases were genuine or not the warders would place the inmates in chains for a few days. Yet the psychiatric hospital was very close to the prison.

I did not realise that a human being could shrink so much that he or she would look like a wasp. I did not know that people could go completely blind with hunger. I did not know that kwashiorkor could make people stop walking. I knew of people passing blood in their urine, of people defecating blood, but not of a human being excreting small balls of faeces like a goat. Until they threw me into this mind-destroying environment.

Marooned in this place as the only political prisoner, I was lonely. Sometimes I would stay up all night in a Yoga

---

* Wole Soyinka, *The Man Died* (London: Rex Collings, 1992).

pose, gazing at the night crawlers: rats that scurried in and out of my cell, spiders and bed bugs that were bold enough to disregard my presence. Roaches and more roaches. Roaches that came straight from the open sewer behind my cell. I would think of Wole Soyinka, the imprisoned writer in *The Man Died**, who held talks with the roaches in his solitary confinement. *How did he pull through*? *He made friends of roaches, ants and mice!* When the geckos stayed close to the dim electric light bulb in the ceiling to catch midges, I would sometimes think that they were watching over me. Since Ihagh did not let me use a mosquito net (he said I could hang myself with it!), I had to arrive at a truce with the new breed mosquitoes. They could suck as much blood as they wanted as long as they stopped waking me up. The result was fatal. Just like Babangida and Abacha, they usually forgot the conditions of the loan. I was forced to buy and take chloroquine injection every month.

The barking of dogs, the mooing of cattle, the bleating of sheep and the crowing of cocks in the neighbourhood always heralded the dawn of a new day. And the howl of some birds, which I could not quite place, plus the chirping of some happy crickets, often signaled the beginning of nights. I was not allowed a wristwatch (the authority said I could kill myself with it as well!), but so accurate was outer nature in its own measurement of time that I had no regrets. I was not allowed to read until I lodged a complaint with the Comptroller (the immediate successor to Aghi) who said why not? Even then, I was only allowed fiction, *The Holy Qur'an* and *The Holy Bible*. Other conditions were imposed on me. Discussing politics with warders or any inmates was strictly forbidden. It was a serious offence to write my friends. I was banned from reading newspapers and magazines. I was barred from listening to the radio. His boss had to order Ihagh before he sewed a long sleeve shirt and a pair of trousers for me in August 1996. It was not that

Ihagh was playing by the rules. By making things difficult, he wanted to force me to pay in cash for whatever little convenience I got in jail.

Ihagh did not allow me to cook my own food until I gave him some money. The day he was going to give me the permission he called me to his office and said,

'The Bible says do not muzzle an ox when you are using it to thresh corn.'

'What do you mean by that?' I asked.

He rolled his eyes. Ticking off his fingers, he mimed a request for money. No quibbling about the price. He knew that Obasa and my friend Segun Adeyemo had dropped some money in the Records for my welfare. I looked genuinely bewildered. With my back to the wall, I gave in. We shook hands on this. I later learnt that he requested for some gallons of paint which Obasa quickly supplied. He even specified the quality of the paints he wanted: nothing but auto-based. For him, prison was not just a penal institution; it was an *industry*. Even when the Comptroller-General had outlawed the gang system, Ihagh still sent prisoners out for cheap labour.

I ate very little, but I was very mindful of what I ate because I was afraid of being poisoned. Yam, beans, rice, *kunun**, fish and oranges were the food I kept alternating. It was on September 26, 1997 that Chief Superintendent of Prisons (CSP), Wuyep Gwali, who succeeded Ihagh, allowed me to use a kerosene stove. Before then, I used firewood, just like the rest of the yard. He also gave me a rickety bed, a new 6 by 2 mattress, and I was allowed to buy a mosquito net.

---

* Corn meal.

Following the international outcry that attended the hanging of the Ogoni 9 and our case, the regime of Abacha began to relent. After five excruciating months of isolation, it sent a memo that I should submit two names of people I would like to visit me in jail. I sent the names of my wife, whom I knew would give me news from home, and Obasa, who would keep me abreast of the news from our company. But Obasa had to assume my surname in order to visit as my cousin, then I began to suffer anew. Apart from the surveillance mounted on them, the meetings were conducted in the office of the man in charge.

Whenever Obasa was so frustrated, he would say to me in Yoruba,

'What security do they think they have here? But for the fact that people would think you committed the offence, we could invade this place and release you!'

We were not allowed to discuss any other thing besides my welfare, and the money they brought. But we broke the ban many times by talking politics in Yoruba. Obasa and Bunmi were generally liked in Makurdi Prison because the two of them were quite generous. I had little or nothing to give. I was simply a beneficiary of their give-aways.

A week after a visit I would begin to look forward to having another one. I would long for the warmth of my wife. I would long for the hassles of the newsroom itself. I would long to father my little kids. Each time I listened to the children across the wall telling their moonlight tales, nostalgia and grief would overcome me. Their tender voices would remind me of my own children, and the innocence of other children of our country. *What would be the future of Nigeria for them with an ill-educated leader like Abacha in power?*

The day Bunmi brought Folarinwa, our new baby, I was a very happy prisoner. I held the child to my chest and prayed for him. I could not stop looking at this healthy boy. I wanted to hug my wife but the warders did not let me. Such moments, I realised that it is when you are incarcerated that you realise that freedom is priceless. Freedom in which to earn independence, dignity and self-respect.

I would react with severity to insult one day and at another I would be meek like a dove. The authority, for that reason, was never certain where it stood with me. As I endured the contumely of warders, I suffered from other hails of anxieties as well: *Is there any terrible news that Bunmi and Obasa are keeping from me? Are the warders coming to search my cell? Are they going to transfer me to another prison at a moment's notice? Are they going to sneak poison into my food? Could they ask a warder on night duty to kill me, my window is always open and he has the key to my door*!
Under intense observation, I suffered persecution complex. Thinking about it now, there were certain extra care I had to take in all my efforts to smuggle out my numerous notes to my friends on the outside that were really beyond the border of normalcy. A sizable chunk of these notes were scribbled nocturnally and were smuggled out with all the jitters of being caught in the act. No matter how you try to stay calm in prison, no matter how you try not to be distressed and frightened, you cannot escape the kind of fear that prison brings. They once had orders to search my cell. But they did not find my full diaries and notes. In anger, they removed my mattress from the floor. What did they find? Pebbles.

In February? In March? I don't recall the precise date. I remember it was hot and stifling. An enormously frustrating moment. Agah, a senior warder, was introducing twelve warders-in-training to the prisoners. As he got to my cell, he banged the door and began, 'Although this cell is meant for the condemned prisoners but this convict is a coup plotter....'

I flared up.

'You must be very stupid. If you don't know what to say why not shut up.'

They were all shocked.

I had not had a fight since I was brought to jail. The man was surprised. He broke into Tiv then switched to English again.

'I will hang my rank today. How can a common criminal insult me like that?' He reported to Dugbe, the new Keeper.

I was led to the Keeper's office where all the warders on the morning shift were waiting. I saw that they were ready to show me the power of little men.

'How did it happen?' Dugbe wanted me to tell the gathering.

'He is a warder. He can say anything. I am a common criminal. Am I not? I am condemned to silence. Let cowards like him take advantage of this circumstance. I won't say anything until I see the man in charge of this prison.'

I knew the new Chief Superintendent of Prisons, Wuyep Gwali, was not in, but prisoners were not supposed to know. Caught in a quandary, Dugbe said I should be returned to the cell.

Case closed? Not yet.

The following morning, Gwali summoned me to his office. He appealed to me to regard my imprisonment as a passing phase. He said he prayed for me everyday and that I would soon go home. He accused the warder who had come to my cell of being overzealous. The warder apologised. We hugged each other, and I in turn said I was sorry for being rude to him. Case closed.

'I am digging for gold. Digging. Digging. Digging. Digging for gold.' The noise was so deafening that midnight. It woke up many of the inmates. The noisemaker: the madman, who was brought to Makurdi Prison for stealing some clothes belonging to his brother's wife. He was locked up in the punishment cell. With all the shackles on, he dug the floor of the cell with his fingers.

'Nobody should join me. If you join me, I will break your legs.'

The warders on night duty laughed.

'Mathias. Mathias. My boy. Bring my food. With a lot of meat. I don't want water. Only wine.'

In the dead of night. Again, the warders laughed and laughed.

The following morning, he was dragged out of the cell on the orders of the man in charge. Thinking that the madman was pretending, the officer ordered that he should be flogged. He then asked the madman,

'Do you know me?'

'Yes, I know you.' The madman replied.

'From where?'

'I know you, now'.

'Who am I?' the Chief Superintendent of Prisons asked with a lot of airs.

The madman had to think for a while. Then he said, 'You are a tout.'

The officers dispersed. They had confirmed that truly Abraham was mad.

They tied him to one of the trees in the yard like a dog. I was traumatised by the frequent beatings he got. His eyes wet with tears, he would always mumbled in Igbo. There was nothing I could do to stop the beating. And that was the most painful part. The madman was eventually freed by Justice Idoko the then Chief Judge of Benue State who, as a ritual, came to prison every year to grant this kind of amnesty.

It was reassuring to receive a mass of letters and postcards every week from all over the world. Many of the warders began to treat me with more respect and affection when those letters began to arrive. The letters were from members of PEN, Amnesty International and other human rights organisations. The most prolific of them were Akira Abe and Hiroko Saso in Japan, Myriam Verwiel and Nynke Steunebrink in Holland and Anne Sebba in London, Elizabeth Zila in Sweden, Agneta Pleijel in Stockholm, Edith Sommer in Vienna, J. Chamberlain in Hong Kong and Deirdre Haslett in Ireland. Many of my compatriots also wrote. The messages were so moving that I would read and reread them. To be loved in that hostile environment by so many people around the globe was like a soothing balm. Let me share with you the joy of reading some of those letters again:

Dear Kunle,

Long time. I got your note on my mother's death. Thanks a lot for the kind words. Please, be assured that you are uppermost in our prayers to the Divine always. We hope that, very soon, this nightmare will be over.

We are struggling to keep afloat— things are terribly bad outside here. The economy continues to suffer depression. We'll continue to do our best to ensure that we all survive to write the story of this terrific time of our nation.
Toyin and Tobi send greetings—very warm greetings.
Don't let your spirit waiver.

My warmest regards,
Bayo Onanuga.

My dear Kunle,

How is your health? I put my trust in God Almighty that He will protect you. By now you should have received my last letter in which I wrote that it was necessary to move to another house. Now we have relocated. Messrs Sola Akinboade, Adeolu Ademoyo, Sola Olorunyomi and Dr. Remi Raji all helped with the tedious relocation. They really surprised me: they worked hard. Our uncles too came around despite their heavy workload.

Dipo (my younger brother) got married on April 19th. We were in Ilesha for the traditional marriage—the wife is from Ilesha. She also went to the Obafemi Awolowo University. She works in Lagos.

We all miss you. Stay blessed, creative and very confident in the knowledge that many people are behind you.
Your dear wife,
Bunmi.

Our dear Kunle,

More than a year of silence has gone by. But you remain cherished always. We feel your pain, but we also note that you don't feel crushed.

A flood of memories cascades our brains as we remember the ties that bind. It is hard to contemplate failure when we remember what we all owe you.

This much we say: that you remain a man beloved whatever our foes say or do. I write in the hope that you are permitted sufficient space to record your experiences. We all need the book when the dark days are gone.

Preserve yourself, it is crucial to earn a chance to laugh last.
Cheers.
Muyiwa Adekeye.

Dear Kunle,
Happy New Year and all our love and greetings. There's so much to say but let me limit it to the greetings and love from Ifekitan, Aramide, Husseina, Nana, Ola and Arinola Fajemisin, Mr. & Mrs. Odebiri (in Ilorin), Akin Olorunyomi and many more.
Take care.
Ladi Olorunyomi.

Dear Kunle,
Wishing you God's blessings and protection in these trying times. I know our good and merciful God will always take care of you until we meet soon. Kunle, please, remember one of your great essays before this ordeal, "Of Solitude and Salman Rushdie." I never forget the interesting way you meditated that the ingenuity of man blossoms in times of solitude. Your situation is not different from those who must suffer for their thoughts to endure. I know and trust my God that He will bring you back home safely. We all love you Kunle, so please be cheerful because your loved ones are waiting for you.

Your Friend,
Dele Kuku.

Odia Ofeimun smuggled in a note with the intention to draft me for service in literature:

Our dear Kunle,

I'm writing this in a bus on my way to meet Obasa at work. For now do me a favour: can you, from memory, write a 2,500 word essay on each of 20 African writers that you have interacted with; to move from their persons to their books and what you think of the relationship between their public roles and the views projected by their books. It's like asking you to rewrite from memory some of your critical pieces and reviews—with an extra: How would you introduce say; Wole Soyinka, Gabriel Okara, Cyprian Ekwensi, Mabel Segun, Atukwei Okai, Biodun Jeyifo, John Munonye, Wale Ogunyemi, Zainab Alkali, Bode Sowande, Oyin Ogunba, Micere Mugo, Ama Ata Aidoo, Chinweizu, Laolu Ogunniyi, Chukwuemeka Ike, Adebayo Williams, Ifeoma Okoye, Tess Onwueme, Elechi Amadi, Emmanuel Obiechina, Olu Oguibe, Funso Aiyejina, Abiola Irele, Olu Obafemi, Karen King-Aribisala, Naguib Mahfouz, etc. etc. to a grown –up Mayowa who needs to know more than what books, their books, can tell about the authors. Out of 20 writers of your choice, make sure there are at least five women.

I am not pretending that memory is easy. Memory is rehearsal, ritual and re-presentation. Perhaps remembering some little encounter with one writer may help you put a seal on how they must be interpreted. The point is to write them as stories, not criticism. The future is for those who have the patience and good sense to have conversations and arguments with yesterday and today. But always remember that stories last longer than arguments. No one can defeat a well-told story.

Thank your God for being who and what you are by celebrating the world you know and what you have shared with your fellow human beings. I'm sure you won't ever have to regret the hardships of the moment. Like gold that you go through mud to bag, the good must teach you to forget the mush. Your day of freedom is not when you are free from the physical chains of the jailer; it is the moment you seize, the day you seize for yourself in a story that out-lasts your jailers and every jailer.

Think good things about yourself and everything that beats the dark days away.

Sincerely,
Odia.

Although I appreciated his concern for the health of my mind, I rebuked Ofeimun: *why do you imagine that I'm on a writing fellowship?* He retreated gracefully only when I promised that I would guarantee the immortality of my stories by writing them magnificently.

An encouraging note from my minder in London:

Dear Kunle,
I wanted you to know that we were all thinking of you last week as PEN organised an evening of reading called "In Praise of Freedom", and we read a piece of your writing. Your name was in The Times. This painting is a dream—I hope you still dream of freedom.

Your friend,
Anne Sebba.

From Aberdeen in Scotland this moving message:

Dear Mr. Ajibade,
When Nigeria gained its independence in 1960 it was my great privilege to be living and working in Ibadan. As

the Principal of the School of Nursing at the University College Hospital I participated in the celebrations at that time and share the aspirations and expectations of your fellow countrymen that Nigeria would continue to develop and flourish as a healthy, prosperous and honourable country— to be a fine example of true democracy to the whole of Africa and beyond.

Sadly we know and regret that this is not so. I salute your courageous efforts for justice and promotion of human rights and urge you to hold fast to your hope and belief that democracy will return to Nigeria and that rights will prevail.

Your imprisonment is a violation of your citizenship—I trust and pray that this wrong will speedily be ended and that you will regain your freedom soon.

May God be with you. Shalom—in peace.

Yours Sincerely,

Isabel Fimister

And from Japan, another useful contact with caring humanity:

Dear Kunle,

How are you? Today (Jan. 15th) is a holiday, called Seijin-no-hi. Young people become adults when they turn twenty. Seijin-no-hi is for their day. I sent you many letters and some books last year. Are you allowed to read them? Whatever happens, I will never surrender. Of course, I am not a Kamikaze suicide pilot! I will continue letter-writing tenaciously this year.

All best wishes to you.

Sincerely yours,

Akira Abe.

From Los Angeles Larry Siems wrote:

Dear Kunle,
On behalf of my 1,000 colleagues here at PEN Center USA West, I send you my best regards, deepest respect, and solidarity. May 1998 bring celebratory headlines !

From Copenhagen I got this message:

Dear Colleague,
Please receive the attached book as an expression of our support and solidarity and as a contribution to better your access to the written word. We hope that the book will please and suit your needs, apologising in advance if it does not, as we unfortunately do not know neither your preferences nor your needs. Danish PEN will be happy to hear from you and learn about your situation. We hope that this can be the start of a strong and friendly relation.
We wish you all the best.
Yours Sincerely,
Jorgen Knudson
President of Danish PEN

From New York, PEN American Center wrote:

In celebration of International Human Rights Day, December 10, 1997, we send you our best wishes for a New Year filled with Hope and Freedom.

From Sweden came this note:

Dear Kunle Ajibade,
Although we have never met and do not know each other personally, I still would like to send you my greetings on the edge of this New Year of 1998, as well as my burning hope

for a better future, and my great respect.

Yours Sincerely,
Agneta Pleijel
Swedish writer.

And finally, these two tender notes from Holland:

Hello Mr. Ajibade,

I am seven years old. This colour is the colour of our country's flag. Today we remember our freedom from the Second World War. In our family we decided to think of people who are not free now. We believe in Jesus Christ who tells us to remember people in prison as if we're in prison with them.

Lots of love.
Anne Roos.

Dear Kunle,

I am Marjoloin, and I live in Holland. I am 13 years old. I will only say to you: my best wishes and hopes for your freedom are with you. Take heart from knowing that you are not forgotten!

The Comptroller of Prisons in Benue State, Albert Sa'ad, withheld my mail until I wrote him a letter which he considered irreverent. Because I had been reliably informed that there was no order from anywhere banning me from reading my mail, I asked the Comptroller to let me have them without any further delay. By way of concluding the letter I wrote:

'I know the constraints under which you people work in respect of our case. But you should at least be a little creative in the way you apply all the draconian orders from the headquarters, knowing full well that things are not cer-

tain. All the informed viewers of current events in our coun-
try know that the evil that is dominating now will only last
for a while. When the lunacy that is impersonating reason
is decisively dealt with, I only hope that people like you will
not suffer regret. I will still like to hold a meeting with you
in order to straigthen out all other matters pertaining to
the terrible conditions under which I am being kept.'

Upon receiving that letter which I wrote on April 1, 1997,
the furious Comptroller rushed down from his own office. In my
presence, he tonguelashed Ihagh, saying that his prison was too
porous. He then brought out the note I had written to him, read
out the bit on 'the lunacy that is impersonating reason.'

'If I send this note to Abuja, it is you who would regret what
you have done, not me.' He fiddled with his rank as if he wanted
to call my attention to it. He then said I should sit down on one
of the two cushion chairs in the small office of Ihagh. I refused
his offer. He asked me why. I told him that prisoners like me
were not allowed to sit on the cushion chairs in this office.

He looked at Ihagh for confirmation, but Ihagh kept silent.
The Comptroller then said,

'I order you to sit on the chair'.

I obeyed.

'Who told you I was keeping your parcels?' he asked.

I did not say anything. He continued.

'One of the greatest offences in prison is trafficking. This
offence can lead to the dismissal of whoever must have told
you. But if you tell me I will only warn the offender; I won't
dismiss him or her'.

I was truly amused at the irrational way history was repeating
itself. What I refused to do under the threat of a gun, this fellow
expected done because he carried a baton. I was surprised at
his inability to see the futility of his frantic mission. He did not

even have the loyalty of his staff.

'No, I won't tell you', I said briskly.

Ihagh then proposed absurdly to his superior officer that they should bring in the police to torture some suspected officers! This proposal was turned down. I was returned to the cell. The result of that encounter was the deluge of letters. The Comptroller felt humiliated, and he took it out on Ihagh, who made the matter a subject of a lengthy harangue at the parade ground the following day. He warned his staff to be careful with me because I had committed the worst offence in Nigeria.

'If you don't want to die, don't be friendly with that coup plotter. You know me. I won't hesitate to hand over any of you to the soldiers if anything happens.'

I was not bothered when many of the warders deliberately avoided me like a leper. I was very pleased that I had made my point.

At least the pleasure of reading those letters was more than the pain of the warders' denigrating comments. By the middle of March 1998 the last count was 8,740. I had enough time in the world to count them. *All these tributes for doing so little*? I felt so humbled by the generosity and warmth of those who sent those messages. Abacha and his minions took away my liberty, but they did not succeed in taking away my voice. If those letters helped to keep me sane, my replies to some of them gave me a happy feeling of triumph. The credit for that must always go to those prison staff who were secretly on my side.

Two contraband items were tucked under my pillow in March 1997 by a warder. They were newspaper cuttings of *The Punch* of May 28, 1996 and *The Guardian* of Sunday February 16, 1997. The first was a lecture which Dr. Olatunji

Dare was not allowed to deliver on May 23, 1996 at the NUJ House in Somolu, Lagos, to mark my one-year in prison. The second was a poem written by Professor Niyi Osundare for me. I was so bouyed up by the note of optimism the two pieces carried in spite of the representations of the travails of the country, which was their major concern.

Dare, the award-winning columnist, wrote, after a careful survey of the pains and pleasures of journalism: 'As I see it, the press can play no better role at this time than to speak truth to power—to tell those who are forever seeking to build new worlds that life is not a preparation for living but is to be lived as fully as possible, from one moment to the next; to point out that when thought is rendered socially hazardous, people spend more time worrying about the hazard than they do in cultivating their thoughts, that in such a state of affairs, society is the loser.' He did not stop at that. He said that if the Nigerian press operated with a remarkable degree of autonomy, it was not because the authorities were benevolent. Rather it was because, for the most part, the unofficial press would not be cowed or bought.

He agreed that the press has its faults, like all other institutions. 'All too often, it mirrors the ethnic, political and religious cleavages in society when it should seek to rise above them. Sometimes, it is even held captive by these cleavages. By not displaying a keen sense of discrimination, it often confers status on persons that are better ignored. By engaging in selective condemnation of wrong-doings, it compromises its moral stature. Sloppy reporting and writing raise problems of credibility. If a newspaper cannot get basic facts right, why should anyone trust its judgement or insights? But that is no justification for harassment that the press has been subjected to in recent years.'

He noted that with all its faults, the press was still one of the best institutions in Nigeria. 'If some other institutions formally invested with far greater power than the press were only half as dutiful as the press, Nigeria would be a far better country'.

The poem by Osundare, captured the climate of fear and blood into which Nigeria had descended. I succumb to the temptation of reproducing the poem here:

For Kunle Ajibade

1

The harmattan has closed another year

With a blinding haze and dust of fear

In every speck a flurry of fret

Heavy with grief, raw with threat.

I see the moon bleed across the skies

A pale eyebrow with a socket of sighs

The sun holds a whip in its fiery hand

On our naked backs its crimson brand.

The grass, so lean, no longer sings

Even as thorn bushes parade their stings

The earth which once caressed our feet

Sprawls aghast, riddled by heat.

Its sweet song broken by the General's fire

The forest lies limp like logs in a pyre

The land darkens into a graveyard of ashes

On the nation's face a plague of rashes.

Another year, dear brother, has come and gone

The land groans, still, under the yoke of the

gun

The country remains a barrack of fright

Drained of its dreams, deprived of its right.

(Refrain; change of voice/tune)

The country is a lie

Told with a crooked eye

By power-pimps

And their cannibal imps.

Reason is treason

Reason is treason

Truth being so out of season

Treason is reason

11

The gallows are busy, the gaols are full

Death comes easy—by push or pull

Chained and shackled like common slaves

We drop in our prime into the tyrant's graves

Reason is treason— a capital crime

In our jungle of silence, untouched by time

Dump decrees ferociously medieval

In a dark, dense dump so primeval

The streets are red with hired killers

A life for a penny—it's all for thrillers

With delicious bullets fill the dissident mouth

It's the Emperor's ploy from north to south.

The Emperor's fart chokes the nation's nose

But for pimps of power it's sweet as rose

Praise-singers are fat, Truth is lean

To think of cabal so maimed and mean!

(Refrain)

Reason is treason

In the Emperor's season

The nation dangles aloft like a rotten fruit

On the tree of sin in the garden of a brute.

111

This, once again, is the season of Terror

Fed and fortified by a native error

Of tribes who hardly see beyond the surface

Without reason's caution, without a face.

Tyrants take their turns on the nation's throne

To a violent wind all that's good is thrown

A hyena snarls in a rocky palace

To keep the future in peril, the people in place

The country is a lie

Told with a crooked eye

A huge, unsteady monster with parts so uneven

A few born to rule, the rest to be driven

Usurpers fester in pomp and power

Decreeing death and ruin every hour

The favoured man who swept the polls

Is dumped in gaol in a mockery of roles.

And yet every minute the country prays
Without repentance, deeper in crime
Praying and praying while the hyena preys
In tongues devoid of reason and rhyme.
A blistering blow for a land so blessed
With a gang of rulers ever so cursed
A land with abundant honey and milk
Is ravaged like worms without their silk.

1V

Rest your soul, long missed friend
We'll rescue this land from its goggled fiend
To suffer so much without a sin
Is an act most painful, a hellish thing

I holed up, devouring books. Reading was the only means I used to lubricate and preserve my mind from shrinking to fit the smallness of Makurdi Prison. Books gave me the necessary energy with which I pushed against the silence and gloom imposed upon me. Was it the prison atmosphere, or my new outlook on life, that made the writings of some of the authors I read yield different meanings? I read and re-read Toni Morrison, Wole Soyinka, Kenzaburo Oo, William Faulkner, James Baldwin, Pat Barker, Pablo Neruda, Femi Osofisan, Ngugi wa Thiong'o, Chenjerai Hove, V.S. Naipaul, Isaac Bashevis Singer, Festus Iyayi, Joseph Conrad, Chinua Achebe, D.O. Fagunwa, Ayi Kwei Armah, George Orwell, Salman Rushdie, Niyi Osundare, Nadine Gordimer, Kole Omotoso, Tolstoy, Syl Cheney Coker, Vikram Seth, Akinwumi Isola, Hermann Hesse, Alexander Solzhenitsyn, Oladejo Okediji, Vasco Pratolini,

Dostoevsky, Alice Walker, Odia Ofeimun, Nuruddin Farah, Dambudzo Marechera, Edward Said, Adewale Maja-Pearce, Ben Okri, Harry Garuba, Remi Raji, Isidore Okpewho, Dennis Brutus, Sembene Ousmane, Adebayo Faleti, D.H. Lawrence, Gabriel Garcia Marquez, Albert Camus, Isabel Allende, Ola Rotimi, Breyten Breytenbach, Kofi Anyidoho, Tanure Ojaide, Susan Sontag and Carlos Fuentes, among others.

Engrossed in the lonely activity of communing with authors, there were many days I did not bother to leave my cell. This innocuous incident was a source of worry for the warders. They reported me, claiming that my intention was malevolent. They obviously suspected that I was into other things except reading. The non-fictional books I read illegally included Robert B. Reich's *The Work of Nations*, Daniel Yergin's *Prize*, Paul Kennedy's *Preparing for the Twenty-first Century*, Aung San Suu Kyi's *Freedom From Fear, Susan Sontag's On Photography*, Martha Gellhorn's *The View From The Ground* and John F. Kennedy's *Profiles in Courage*. Apart from the books sent by Mrs Gbemi Tejuoso of Glendora in Lagos and the ones sent by my friends in the Netherlands, New York, Japan, Canada and London, my wife also brought a lot of books from my library.

To keep myself physically fit, I walked up and down my cell 500 times every morning and the same times every evening except on Saturdays and Sundays when I did 300 press-ups and 500 pull-aparts.

On August 2, 1997, when the death of Fela Anikulapo-Kuti was announced, the entire prison was shaken to its very foundation with dirges and many of Fela's songs, particularly *Shuffering and Shmiling* and *ITT*. I saw some of those hardened criminals weep. I was told that the free world was ɛngaged in deep mourning for one of the Africa's foremost artistes, a thorn in the flesh of military dictatorship whose *Zombie* is a favourite of a lot of people. In 1984, he was finally jailed by the military Exchange Control Anti-Sabotage Tribunal after many attempts had been made to repress him. He came out of jails more resolutely committed to unfettered freedom to criticise the unrelieved irresponsibility of Nigeria military officers in government. If Fela was (and is still) wildly celebrated for the content of his music, it was not because he said what other people ignored, it was because he did so in an enchanting form that was uniquely his own.

Terry, young and handsome, was giving me a hair-cut with a razor blade and a small comb. Abruptly, he stopped. He said he wanted to tell me something. He had been one of my reliable informants since he had been brought from Otukpo in September 1997. He was condemned to death four years ago. I could not wait for this piece of information.

'Journalist, forget it. It's not important.'

'Do they want to move me to another prison?'

'No, it's not about you'.

'Is it about the warders or your cellmates?'

'No.'

Brief silence. A warder passed by. He then said calmly, 'They will hang me next week.'

He told me that he had dreamt about his hanging the night before. I thought he was joking. But they led him away in chains three days later to Jos Prison because there was no gallows in Makurdi Prison. He was hanged as soon as they got there. I fell into helpless silence. Terry had killed a man during a robbery.

---

¹ From *Resistance, Rebellion and Death* edited and translated by Justin O' Brien (New York: Alfred A. Knopf, Inc., 1960).

I could hear Albert Camus saying in his brilliant piece, *Reflections on the Guillotine,* that 'if murder is in the nature of man the law is not intended to imitate or reproduce that nature. It is intended to correct it'.*

Obasa remembered vividly the invasion of our office on Monday, April 6, 1998. It was 2:00 PM. They were about to start an editorial meeting when Wole Odofin, the Press Manager, rushed in. Agitated, he said, 'They have surrounded Fagba!' Obasa, Akinyemi Onigbinde and Sani Kabir ran out because they knew that after Fagba, which was where one of our offices was located, the police would invade 24 Hours Press, where the editorial meeting was going to be held. They ran to the 4th floor of the next building, which was under construction. Babajide Fatogun, our production consultant, scampered into one of the corners to hide. Within seconds the whole of Acme Road, where the press was located, was under police surveillance. There was chaos everywhere because the police came in about five vehicles and patrolled the whole area. 100 metres to the danger zone, Ofeimun quicky made a U-turn as Adetoun Amidu signalled to him to turn back. He escaped just like Kabir, Onigbinde and Obasa. The police vandalised the office in Fagba, carted away the computers, arrested Lateef Mufutau, Patrick Aigbe, Austin Uganwa, Kehinde Adeyemi, Wole Odofin, Yomi Osoba, Anthony Nwanah and James Ayoola.

Before this raid, the anti-terrorism squad led by Biu had taken over the case of Ojudu who had been arrested by the SSS since November 17, 1997. One morning in March 1998, they drove him to Alagbon where he was made to face a panel of five detectives. They wanted to know where our press was.

Ojudu hesitated. Biu threatened him with a gun. Because Ojudu did not cooperate with them they returned him to the cell in the evening. They brought a photographer who took five shots of him.They also used a video camera. It was as if they had arrested a terrorist. They ordered that nobody should talk to him, or come near him. They put a sticker on his door indicating that it was a danger zone. Ojudu then wondered, *What do these people think I am? Something other than a journalist*?

I felt a lump in my throat when I finished reading Obasa's note. I assured myself, 'This too shall pass!'

A bacha was unrelenting. Like a pariah dog he prowled nervously in the mangrove of the world looking for friends, but his search was futile. Buffeted by the demand for our release, he made promises, which he never kept. The UN, the European Union, the Commonwealth and many non-governmental organisations kept demanding for democracy and an end to the abuse of human rights. The more the appeal, the more determined and angry Abacha became. In the second year that he was a dictator, he began to have a snug illusion that he had conquered the people. He also stole more money from the kitty, using Abubakar Bagudu, Gilbert Chagoury, Mark Rissar, his children and a few others as pointsmen. Some of the money he spent to launder his image abroad. His regime registered five political parties. Incredibly, these political parties soon met and declared him as the consensus candidate for the forthcoming presidential election. The tide of protest that greeted that season of political prostitution led to the arrest of more people.

As tyranny held the nation in its grip, the jails were full of political prisoners. Our country was now too small to contain the grief and fear of many people, a lot of whom had surrendered to cynicism and despair. The country become an excruciating boil waiting to burst. On June 4, 1996, Kudirat Abiola, who was championing the cause of the release of her husband, was killed by assassins, in broad daylight, in the streets of Lagos. Yar'Adua was found stone dead in his cell in Abakaliki Prison on December 8, 1997*. Any news of the death or arrest of people who were pivotal to the struggle against the tyranny of Abacha was a dampening stroke to me in jail.

Abacha was bent on succeeding himself. Daniel Kanu's Youths Earnestly Ask for Abacha (YEAA) had organised an Aso Rock-induced two million man-march in Abuja. The crowd, I was told, included many well-known Nigerians who had claimed in the past that they were democrats. No one stopped Kanu's carnival. Yet the counter-gathering organised in Lagos by Agbakoba, Mrs. Ayo Obe, Abdul Oroh and other activists (which was massively attended) was violently dispersed by the security forces. Even though the wounded Agbakoba was jailed soon after the fiery dispersal, the Lagos gathering succeeded in showing that the self-succession bid by Abacha did not have the support of the majority of Nigerians. Nigerians were no longer docilely surrendering to repression.

Difficult to imagine an end to my torment, I said to myself one morning: *Forget about Abacha and his hardline inanities. Your survival is the only important thing now. Face the fact that you are going to be here for a long time. Map*

---

* For the long list of the dead and many Nigerians put in jail, see Olawale Oshun's *The Open Grave: NADECO and the struggle for Democracy* (Josel Publishers, London, 2002) and Joe Igbokwe's *Heroes of Democracy.* (Clear Vision Limited, Lagos, 1999)

* I was happy to learn that M.D Yusuf, Dr. Iyorchia Ayu, Colonel Abubakar Dangiwa Umar, Dr. Alex Ekwueme and Alhaji Abubakar Rimi, among others, were now telling Abacha to quit.

out a feasible academic programme that will keep you busy within the period. But I could only shut off my mind from Abacha's self-succession plan for just a couple of weeks. I learnt that Soji Omotunde, Obiora Chukwumba, Segun Adeniyi and Mohammed Adamu, all of *African Concord,* had been arrested. Would they ever be left off as quickly as Godwin Agbroko of *THE WEEK* magazine? I was told that, not satisfied with the past incarceration of Nosa Igiebor, the Editor-in-Chief of *TELL*, the SSS had arrested Onome Osifo-Whiskey, the Managing Editor of the magazine. The Kaduna correspondent of the magazine, Danlami Nmodu and Moshood Fayemiwo of the muck raking *Razor* were in detention. Niran Malaolu of *Diet* newspaper had also been arrested for allegedly supporting the Diya's coup by concealing it.

The siege on our offices was so intense: the disappearance of Kaltho, the Kaduna correspondent of *TheNEWS* and *TEMPO;* the detention of Jenkins Alumona, Tokunbo Fakeye, Ben Adaji and Rafiu Salau; the constant harassment of Ladi, the wife of Olorunyomi, who had to flee the country in the wake of a threat to his life; the arrests of Demola Abimboye, Gbenga Alaketu and Hassan Turaki; and the flight of Onanuga to the US when Major Al-Mustapha, ordered that he should be shot and thrown into the Lagoon. Obasa, who was managing the business in our absence, had started wearing a beard, a cow boy hat and a pair of dark glasses as disguise. He had told his immediate family to vacate his residence. It was clear that the worst was about to happen to Independent Communications Network Limited (ICNL) when Biu sealed up our offices and carted away the computers in April 1998. I was not only upset by all of this, I was also afraid for the people on the outside. It seemed to me then that being in jail was a little respite.

I did not know that my blood pressure had shot up until Dr. Chibuzo Okoro of the Benue State Ministry of Health gave me a check-up. By now, I was smashed to bits psychologically: I could not calm down. I could not teach my adopted prison student, Ahmad Bature, his English lesson. Okoro was worried. I was deeply touched by the humanity of this woman who always insisted in her reports on me that my rights as a political prisoner should not be denied.

I depended on two sources to get current information on political events from outside. The first was Gwadabe, who was then serving a long jail term in Gboko Prison*. The second was Sunday Orinya, our Makurdi correspondent. I gave Orinya the task of sending me the summary of the major stories of the week through our contact. I tried to squeeze information out of Gwadabe each time I wrote to him. I succeeded in getting two cover stories for *TheNEWS* as a result of the rich correspondence between us. Here is one of his letters:

19/9/97

My dear Kunle,

Thanks a lot for keeping in touch. Under the present circumstances, I can't say that I'm doing well. But I always take solace in this James Mitchener's quotation: "They wake each morning to a fresh day that has forgiven the previous day's outrages." I am a little bit pissed off now, but in few days time, I shall get over it.

The death of Maiwada, the man in charge of this prison, has revealed the extent of his monumental corruption. I am amazed at the capacity of human beings for intrigue. Despite his shabby treatment of me here, including road-

---

* They replaced him with Obiki who was now taken to the Maximum Security Prison, Kirikiri.

block tactics against my family, the man extorted so much money from us under one pretense or the other. Yet I helped with the payment of his medical bills. Until I finally encouraged him to do a thorough medical test, he did not know that he had the AIDS virus. That caused him to go on leave on July 18, 1997.

Despite the trauma the man had caused me, the day he died, I went to the front office to see if I could get my funds from his safe to send something to his family. Only to discover that, when he was going on leave, he went with all my money: N54,000. Since nobody here can help me. I decided that as a matter of policy I should always have substantial money here, but that has now proved my waterloo. The former DCP here, Austin Jinge, was removed because he stole my N35,000 for medication and food. Where is the hiding place if I may ask? My family out there is facing trouble from the DMI and in here the wolves in uniforms have not left me in peace.

I lodged a formal complaint to the Comptroller today to see what he can do about it. In fact, I delayed writing this morning to see whether I can send you a copy of my petition because I decided to expose most of the iniquities I had to contend with here. The dead man's constant demands from people frustrated them, that they only came here on occasions. Anytime a demand was not met, the guy would pretend not to be available for visit, while a strict order was given that nobody was to conduct a visit for me except him. My stay with him here from June 1996 till date when he paraded himself as a messiah to right wrongs here, was nothing but a dose of hell.

As usual, you are my 'presidential adviser' on these matters! What do you reckon should be the next step? Hasn't this confirmed that this is a citadel of corruption? The corrupt sent us here after a stick up so that we can be fleeced.

I got a letter from Columbus in which he revealed the graft and the inhumanity in your place there. I was speechless. Unfortunately, he passed the letter thro' the system and the officers were appalled at the happenings in Makurdi Prison even accusing Columbus of fabricating lies. Then a week later, the episode here! They are currently in hiding with shame!

Back to our macabre dance: our man in Abuja is truly ill. Very ill. His liver problem is now at an advanced stage exacerbating his lack of performance. Sometimes he does not go to work for two weeks. During the ECOWAS (Economic Community of West African States) meeting I was told that he looked emaciated. The skin has changed. In effect, I don't believe he has a long way to go. My brother, what did they say about the wicked?

On the international front, a delegation of Caribbean and some Asian leaders are due to meet with Mr. Tony Blair before the Commonwealth Conference in October. Our case is slated for discussion. I will keep you posted.

I am enduring all the way.

L.G.

The phantom coup of 1995 was used to throw out Gwadabe out of the army. He had earlier been sacked as the Principal Staff Officer (PSO) to the Head of State, Abacha. He said it was very frustrating working with Abacha: 'He never cared for channels of communication. He was never a respecter of time. In fact, the man acted as if the whole world must wait for him. He was quite incapable of articulating his own position on any subject even when such positions were made available to him. He did not have a grasp of the problems of Nigeria. His main interest was money. He was obsessed with making money. Yet he was always ruthless in denying others their own entitlements'.

Gwadabe was posted out of the State House to the Gambia. Few months after he got to the place, the military, which he had gone there to train, staged a coup against the civilian government of President Dauda Jawara. Accused of being the spirit behind the revolt, he was recalled home and posted to 23 Armoured Brigade in Yola.

He always wanted to be at the centre of events. When Abacha gave him the job of Director of Customs Services, Gwadabe rejected, preferring to remain in the Presidential Villa. He was one of the officers used by Babangida to topple the regime of Buhari. He was subsequently made the governor of Niger State. He led the troops, which backed up Abacha, Diya and Gusau, that overthrew the Shonekan ING. Abacha used a lot of Gwadabe's contacts to rationalise his coup. As a core northerner with a rising profile in the army, he could pull political strings with a measure of brilliance and persuasiveness for his maximum comforts, and sometimes for the betterment of the country. Conscious of power that he wielded, he was brash and arrogant, even to his superiors. And for that, he became an endangered element.

I had one of the most gut-wrenching moments in Makurdi Prison on May 28, 1998. Chief Bola Ige* was brought from the office of the SSS in Makurdi, where he had been

---

* Upon his release, Ige later became the country's Attorney-General and Minister of Justice in the civilian government of Olusegun Obasanjo, but was murdered on December 23, 2001 by hired assassins.

detained on account of the bloody May Day protest against Abacha in Ibadan, which was fully supported by the United Action for Democracy (UAD) and the Committee for the Defence of Human Rights (CDHR). It turned out to be a riotous protest because one of the properties of Alhaji Azeez Arisekola Alao, an Ibadan businessman, who wanted Abacha to cling to power, was attacked. Impulsively, his thugs descended on some of the notable protesters. It became a free-for-all fight. Some people lost their lives. The regime of Abacha found in this another reason to clampdown on his critics. Ige was one of those critics arrested. While Alhaji Lam Adesina and several others, who were described by the Military Administrator of Oyo State, Colonel Ahmed Usman, as 'prisoners of war' were detained in Agodi Prison, Ige was set aside for a harsher punishment. The plan to burn down his house was not hatched but he was bundled out of Ibadan as if he was going to be killed.

An elderly friend, he had attended the naming ceremony of Folarinwa, my son, in January 1996. I had smuggled out a note thanking him for that kind gesture of standing by my grieving family. For that personal touch, I embraced him in tears as he was led to one of the filthiest cells in the prison: Cell A1. The bed was very old and creaking, the floor was pockmarked and the roof and ceiling leaked. When I finished disinfecting the cell about two hours after his arrival, Ige said, 'the good thing is that I have no sense of smell'.

My other reason for the fellowship of concern had to do with the free education and medical programmes which he carried out as the first executive governor of the old Oyo State under the control of the UPN led by Awolowo. In Makurdi Prison, he drew a line constantly between the politicians hurriedly made by the military whose notable failing is a lack of sense of civic responsibility and a few Nigerian politicians like himself who love to command political events for public good.

Endowed with very good intellect, he narrated the three years of political struggle in my absence with the finesse of an historian who has an abiding interest in politics. He told me that Abacha stopped the launching of his *People, Politics and Politicians of Nigeria (1940-1979)* on April 17, 1996. Ige wrote the book when Buhari kept him in jail between 1984 and 1986.

He also shared with me his views on foreign affairs, mysticism and literature. He would quote several lines of Joseph Conrad off hand to show that Conrad's prose is worth emulating. I did not share his view on Conrad. So we had passionate discussions on creative writing. I told him that Saul Bellow, Gabriel Garcia Marquez, Milan Kundera, Toni Morrison, Salman Rushdie, Mario Vargas LLosa and Carlos Fuentes have extended the frontiers of fiction beyond the limited imagination of Conrad. He preferred Maya Angelou to Toni Morrison. Contrary to popular opinion, he was more enamoured of Demosthenes than Cicero, which is his sobriquet in the Nigerian press.

I was impressed by his stoicism. Ige carried himself with dignity in jail. Some of the warders misinterpreted his carriage for arrogance. One morning, two of the warders on night duty came to report him, saying that he had shouted at them the night before.

'*The man no know say parade don change. He no know say this place no be government house. Make you warn am, well, well. We no sabe book, but we sabe warder job*', they fumed.

'I don't want to give these people any quarter. No, these people won't trample upon me. No, they won't', he later told me.

If there was anything those warders detested, it was the fact that Ige seemingly treated them with absolute scorn.

After a week in Makurdi Prison, he had learnt to tolerate not just the noise from the armed robbery suspects' cell next to him, but also a lot of other demeaning things like taking his bath every evening in the open air. The only thing I could do was to make sure that the water was always warm and sanitised.

For him, a simple diet was the staff of life. He ate cabbage, cucumber, tomatoes, lettuce, onion, carrots, bread, pineapples, oranges, groundnuts and biscuits. The last two he ate as if they were delicacies. I guess because his wife, Justice Atinuke Ige, brought them. He was free to buy all those fruits and snacks because he was a detainee, not a convict like me. He drank four cups of tea without milk everyday: two in the morning, two in the evening. On several occasions, I offered him some pieces of roast meat. Each time I did so, and I always made sure it was on days he was fasting, he would smile and say in Yoruba, '*Esu pada leyin mi*' (Leave me alone, this rascal!). To keep fit, he paced up and down his room many times every morning.

He once told me: 'Those who have put me in jail are empty shells awaiting the bulldozers of history'. One Sunday over a meal of *akara* (bean cake), which I prepared, we had a very interesting debate on Kemal Ataturk who, besides Gandhi, Nehru and Awolowo, he admired a lot. In response to my observation that Ataturk was a philanderer, he asked me rhetorically: 'Did that take away anything from his sense of duty and his honesty as a politician? He smiled as he quoted D.H. Lawrence for emphasis, 'Is love not an inspirational force?'

He reread some of Soyinka's books, not because he was one of the prime associates of Soyinka, but because, according to him, there is a touch of quality in them. 'How scant and timid our literature would be without his contribution,' he said. Ige referred to Soyinka fondly as *Ekeji mi* (My companion). In admiration of Soyinka, he quite often said in Yoruba, '*Wole ti goke agba*' (Wole has really made his mark). Ige was working on two manuscripts in jail: his prison diary and a book of his own reading of the Bible.

He read and wrote everyday. In four uninterrupted hours, he read my copy of Jeffrey Archer's *A Matter of Honour*. He enjoyed reading my smuggled copy of Paul Kennedy's *The Rise and Fall of Great Powers* from which he took copious notes. It was over the Carlos Fuentes's 'A Harvard Commencement', a lecture which the author delivered in 1983 in Harvard University, that we had a most fascinating discussion on the politics of unity and diversity. What triggered off that discussion was this quote from the lecture: '*One of the wonders of our menaced globe is the variety of its experiences, its memories, and its desires. Any attempt to impose a uniform politics on this diversity is like a prelude to death.*'* Ige, who used to preach politics of national cohesion, had been forced by the unrelenting northernisation of the Nigerian polity to modify his position, a position which he said Alhaji Balarabe Musa grossly misunderstood when he tagged him a tribalist. Under the regime of Abacha, aspersions were cast on the Yoruba; they were mocked as many of their children were mowed down in their cities for protesting against injustice. If Ige had not risen to defend his people, he would have been labelled an irresponsible leader.

I give no apology for detailing the books Ige read in prison because this was the aspect of our relationship that continuously fascinated me. Before he came, there was no one to hold any serious dialogue with. I suppose that extensive reading is the root of his cultural sophistication and substantial talent to

---

* Carlos Fuentes, *Myself With Others* (London: Pan Books Limited, 1986).

make a quick connection between the quotidian and the extraordinary, between the domestic and the international. Many of our politicians don't read. It was a privilege to meet this one whose range and depth of reading complimented the time he spent on nurturing his political ambition. Ige treated men of ideas with due respect because, in many ways, he was one of them.

He would constantly plead with me: 'You must continue to have standards and measure yourself against the masters. You must continue to have inviolable points of honour. You must preserve your reputation.' One day, when I was giving him a hair cut and our discussion veered towards Abacha again, he said, 'The man does not know that when a leader turns tyrant he demeans himself.'

Even though he was detained under the obnoxious Decree No.2, 1984, that empowered the Inspector-General of Police to arrest and detain any citizen for six months in the first instance, or indefinitely without trial), he was very optimistic that Abacha would not be allowed to 'transmogrify' himself into a civilian president. He was sure that he would soon go home. He kept drawing from that power of positive thinking.

And Abacha died on June 8, 1998. The warder who had whispered the news to me in the night of that day said he had died like a poisoned rat and had been buried as such. He said even the death of his son, Ibrahim, in a plane crash on January 17, 1996 had some dignity compared to Abacha's. It was one of the greatest pieces of news I have ever had in my life. I began to imagine which appropriate magazine headlines would capture it. I settled for 'The Death of a Crude Tyrant.' I read again Suratul Bakar verse 7 of *The Holy Qur'an*: 'In their hearts is a disease and Allah increaseth their disease. A painful doom is theirs because they lie.' Abacha's legacy to Nigeria consists of assassination squads, a looted state purse and a country more sharply divided along ethnic lines. He made himself inaccessible to reasonable arguments. He reduced Nigeria to a primitive arena of absolute terror.

In the morning, I rushed to Ige's cell to break the news. He asked that we pray for our country. We soon got to know that, at Abacha's death, the jubilant crowd that poured into our nation's unhappy streets was unprecedented in the annals of our history. The dances of joy in the homes of so many people went for a long time. Hilarious voices across the walls hurling enormous curses at Abacha in his grave. The time-honoured theme of good triumphing over evil became a constant refrain in the tongues of artists, journalists and priests. The international community also heaved a deep sigh of relief. It was as if death had ceased to be the soul of tragedy itself.

But how did he die? Was it a palace coup? None of the informants was sure. Ige joined me in my cell for the analysis of all possible fall-outs of Abacha's death. I told Ige that people might not win, even though Abacha had lost the battle. Out of desperation I asked,

'Why is it that our country has never been loved by many of its leaders? Why do they bash it, smash it up all the time?'

Ige said, *'Selfishness. Greed. Betrayal'*. It struck us disturbingly that Abacha's death was just a fragile victory. We were worried that if General Jeremiah Useni became the new Head of State things would certainly take a more tragic turn. We, however, agreed that whoever took over would want to be loved and hailed in the first few weeks of his regime. When the mantle of leadership fell on Abubakar, he promised, as we expected, to look into all the cases of those who were in jail for political reasons.

On June 15, 1998 he ordered the immediate release of Ige, Obasanjo, Anyanwu, Ransome-Kuti, Dasuki, Olabiyi

Durojaiye, Frank Ovie Kokori, Udem Udoh and Milton Dabibi. Two more batches followed but I was not there. I believed I was going to make the next list with Abiola and the others.

As soon as he got to Ibadan, Ige told my wife that he would soon address a press conference on my plight in jail, which he did in a most effective way. When the new Head of State invited him to Aso Rock, Ige reportedly told Abubakar and his Principal Staff Officer, Brigadier-General Leo Ajiborisa, that there was no reason to keep me in jail. The constant message from Ige was, 'All is well'. Exhilaration now mingled with anxiety.

I waited for the turn of events calmly not knowing that the hawks in the new regime had perfected their plot to eliminate Abiola. As we waited with bated breath, Abiola, who had been in jail for more than four years, suddenly died on July 7, 1998 when he was discussing with a delegation of the American government, which included Thomas Pickering and William Twaddel. For this meeting, Abiola was moved from Gado Nasko Barracks to Aguda House in Aso Rock. As the nation was plunged into mourning, I lamented the death of a victim of political intrigues. A victim of military conspirators, some of whom he had helped to nurture and some of whom he had done business with in the past. Once again, wails of separation rang loud in our country. I felt sad for a nation that missed an opportunity to make a giant leap: a nation whose democratic rights were betrayed by some self- serving military officers and their opportunistic civilian allies. But then, I assured myself that *June 12* remains one historic event in which Nigeria discovered what it was and what it ought to be. I grieved for a land of unhappy citizens with bandaged wounds. I hoped the future would relieve and heal us.

NINE

~~~~~~

Homecoming

I jumped out of my cell with a lot of relief on July 20, 1998, when my freedom was proclaimed. After what seemed like an endless wait, the new Head of State gave an order that Sani, Sanusi Mato, Felix Ndamaigida, Charles-Obi, Matthew Popoola, Julius Badejo, Mbah, Moses Ayegba, Rebecca Ikpe and myself should be released from prison. I was told that in the broadcast, in which he announced our release, Abubakar also announced a ten-month transition programme, which would produce a new president on May 29, 1999. But I spent an extra day in jail because the papers for my release were not sent to the Comptroller of Prisons on time. It was an extra day that made me panic. I thought that the government had changed its mind. After all, it had refused to release the military officers. All night long I could not sleep.

That night two of the warders who had done so much in the past to protect me came to my cell. After a long chat about trivial matters, one of them said:

'Journalist, just go home with a spirit of forgiveness. Don't keep any malice against anybody. Forget all the bad things anybody might have done to you since your trouble started. No-body spends time in jail without losing something. The impor-tant thing is that you have not lost your life.'

I thanked the two warders. I then told them that it would not be difficult for me to forgive my jailers, but I would not pardon or condone the evil system they strove strenuously to protect. About two hours later, all the cells rose in unison to sing for me some of the best prison farewell songs, an event coordinated by the two warders. My mind began to weave dreams of free-dom in colourful threads. The process of my release was brisk. The Comptroller, Sa'ad and Nathaniel Nandebe gave me some papers to sign. I was in a hurry. I scribbled my signature with-out reading the documents. I handed over the only property of the prison in my possession: the two long sleeve shirts and trou-sers meant for hardened criminal. I sighed deeply. At long last! It was all over! ALL OVER!! I stared at the place where the portrait of Abacha used to be. It was vacant. *Where now the Iron man, the Khalifa, the Aso Rock god? Dust: A mere mortal. How many people did he destroy? He will remain a nightmare parenthesis in our long and critical history. His relics will never be honoured by decent people.* But will he be honoured in the sight of God? I allow Prophet Muhammad to speak: 'Verily the dearest of men near Allah on the Resur-rection Day and the nearest of them before Him for company will be a just ruler, and verily the most disagreeable of the peo-ple near Allah on the Resurrection Day and one deserving of the most severe punishment among them will be a tyrannical ruler.'* *Allahu Akbar*!

A lot of people waited for about three hours to see me walk out of prison. When I came out, I took a long emotional

---

* From, *Al-Hadis* by Maulana Fazlul Karim, (The Book House: Lahore, 1940.)

look at Makurdi Prison. Since I had not had the opportunity to see properly its surrounding till now, it was a different experience altogether. *So this is how decrepit this place is on the outside? How come I didn't notice this the day I was brought here?* I could see clearly some fishermen hawking fish by the River Benue. *How would they know that I had been their customer these past painful seasons?* I could see some of the kids whose night songs across the wall had sometimes wet my patched soul for undiluted songs. Did they know that they had contributed in a small way to my survival?

I obliged journalists with interviews before I headed to Abuja by road. Along the way, I gulped the air of freedom like a man who had fasted for days. Abuja looked bigger than I had left it. All the new houses made me feel that I had been gone for too long. The splendour of Abuja, which is its location between many rocks, seduced me. Abuja looked serene apparently because it was still largely a civil servant city where official papers were processed and secret political meetings held. A sharp contrast to Lagos. My first night outside of jail was a night of thanksgiving to God who saved me from the evils of those days of lunacy.

I came to Lagos on the first flight. In the plane, I felt like someone who had just leapt over the cold barricade to the blazing sunlight. I was drenched in the warm shower of recollections. But I knew that my free tongue, wounded by a clique of murderers, should heal first, otherwise I would sound like a broken record singing angrily. I rehearsed what I would say to the journalists. I went to the office from the airport. On my way, I noticed that Lagos had not changed. Its pulsating, punching rhythm was still very much alive: Lagos was still a city of many great challenges; a city of threats and furies; a city of fears and hopes.

Landing in Lagos, my next and final destination way home – Ibadan. On our way, Obasa was now free to talk about the organisation in detail.

'Kunle,' he said, 'it took more effort to be able to run an organisation from five different locations, it affected administrative efficiency. To a very large extent, it scared away a number of people who wanted to work for us but did not want to take the risk. Being a good journalist is not the same thing as being willing to go to jail. We lost a lot of money trying to maintain the solidarity period.

He recalled that, 'Before Abacha died, everything was deteriorating. The country was breaking into pieces before our very eyes. We saw that a separation was leading to a divorce and it didn't promise to be an easy divorce'. According to Obasa, we were no longer what we wanted to be. We were no longer what we were. A new agenda had to be set. We started to understand our role in the society differently. We found that it was not just enough to make money. 'Abiola made a lot of money and that didn't stop them from doing what they did to him. The lesson here is that one has to be partisan on the side of progress. I am very happy to say that, during the period, we totally eliminated fear from our lives because we found that it was possible to triumph over the most powerful dictator if you were determined'.

We both agreed that practising journalism under Babangida and Abacha had its own shortcomings. Fairness suffered, regrettably. Not accessing the points of view of some of the people we wrote about was one of the weaknesses of our practice. But who caused that? The military dictators, of course. Liberal democratic values assume that things are run normally, but Babangida and Abacha changed the rule of decency. It would have been unfair to demand compliance from us.

Ofeimun's thought along the same lines: 'No one who was not a *guerrilla journalist* could practise properly without the kind of ambience provided by *guerrilla journalism.* And the so-called *guerrilla journalist* had an edge over the others for one reason. Those who sneered at them always had to follow their lead. They set the agenda in a lot of ways. If other newspapers failed to carry a particular item but the *guerrilla journalist* featured it, it would become public property. Therefore, other newspapers had to try as hard as possible to catch up with the *guerrilla journalists* because, if they didn't, they looked irrelevant. Suffice to say that if there was no *guerrilla journalism,* there probably would not have been an end to the military regime. As more and more people read the newspapers, they literally poured into the struggle. They knew what was happening and therefore could not be easily misled by government propaganda. Mobilisation is not about getting people to come into the street to demonstrate, it is about getting people to have common access to the same kind of information and therefore giving them a tendency to act together whenever they have to act'.

Ofeimun said that he genuinely did not want to be remembered as Abacha's victim because many of his friends were. 'I tried very hard to stay afloat to be able to punch holes in Abacha's head. I always talk about the period as if it was a period I was prepared to waste. To be honest, when I was returning from Britain, I had made up my mind that I would do nothing but help to resist the military in whatever way possible. When I got back home, I took a hard look at the situation and I realised that the best contribution I could make was by writing in particular ways about the way the system was going. I didn't see it like wanting to earn a living. I just wanted to write about things

that would keep the military in its place. If I hadn't that opportunity, I could have gone mad. Gone mad in the sense that I
would have had to do things that were not particularly rational
within the context. I would have had to join people who, for
instance, would want to raise arms to fight the government. I
did not think Nigeria had reached the point where that would
happen. We were getting there by the time Abacha died'.

What is the new agenda now? Obasa believed that the task
before us is to strengthen the institution of free speech, the
institution of democracy, the culture of democracy. 'We have
to strengthen those pillars. We have the tools. We have the
respectability. We have the clout. We have the medium to do
so. If our conscience permits us and our knowledge gives us
the right strength to do it, this is our role. It is my understanding
that in playing this role we will be sufficiently rewarded not just
in terms of the clout that will come from it, but also in terms of
the country that will emerge from it. I tell you: for as long as you
are working on the side of the people, you will sell. That is
what experience has taught us'.

It was a great joy to be back in the comfort of my home,
which my wife had preserved. She had relocated, yet my
library was still intact. Rising to the challenge of my imprisonment, she ran the home as if nothing had happened. She told
me that throughout the first year of my imprisonment, Mayowa
would wake up in the night and ask, *mummy, where is daddy*?

'I was pregnant', she recalled. 'There was nobody to complain to whenever I was disturbed. I felt so lonely in the midst
of people and things. It was a period of extreme difficulty for
me. I was the father, the uncle and the aunt. I suffered silently.
God was my strength. I used to wake up in the night to pray. I
fasted for many days in pregnancy. Carrying the baby itself

was a source of strength. I knew that you would not be happy in prison if I didn't deliver the baby safely. I shed tears at the naming ceremony of Folarinwa. There were so many people. I appreciated their presence, but I just thought that you should have been there to share the joy with me.'

I had listened to people in Lagos talk about her resilience. Now she had confirmed some of what they said. In those days of emotional stress, she appeared calm, and her equanimity impressed a lot of people. I'm still fascinated by her coping capacity, her ability to close her mind to depressing realities. I held her in my arms several times after my release, just to thank her for the sacrifice she made.

About a week or so after my arrival, Folarinwa would not accept that I was his father. 'No, he is Mayowa's father', he always said any time his mother tried to introduce us. He stopped coming to our bedroom as a mark of protest against the intruder. But I eventually won him over with ice-cream.

Because I had become used to the solitude of jail, I found it difficult to relate well to a lot of people who had come to celebrate my homecoming. I just wanted to be alone.

I came to a country waking up from a nightmare. Ojudu who was still wearing a thick beard when we met after our release from different camps of solitude and agony, said:

'Ah, Kunle! I thought we would never meet again?' He reminded me that we were lucky to be alive.

In the war zone that Nigeria had become in my absence, he was one of those arrested and almost killed in detention. He was arrested at 7:30 PM on November 17, 1997 as he was trying to sneak into Nigeria through the Ghana-Togo border. The SSS trailed him from Cotonou and caught up with him at a checkpoint in Badagry.

'They stopped us, asked all of us to come down, picked me out of the group and took me to a booth where they found out that I work for *TheNEWS*.

They took him to a house in Badagry, their operational base, and kept him there till midnight while they tried to make contact with their head office in Lagos. Because he was afraid that he had been marked for elimination, Ojudu had discretely given his complimentary card to other Nigerians who were in the same booth with him when he was arrested. One of them had been kind enough to tell our office about his arrest.

He was hungry and exhausted. That night, four armed men took him in a jeep to the SSS office in Shangisha and then to the headquarters at Awolowo Road, where his luggage was searched and an inventory taken; his address book, tape recorder, comlimentary cards and the conference papers. His cellmates included Jenkins Alumona of *TheNEWS*, Ogaga Ifowodo and Akin Adesokan: two of the young award-winning Nigerian writers who had earlier been arrested at the Seme border. Ojudu was interrogated the next day by the Lagos State Director of SSS. NO. It was not an interrogation. It was a rowdy session of abuse.

He recalled, 'I became angry and shouted at the SSS Director: Look, you are supposed to be interrogating me. I am the one who allegedly committed an offence, what has my ethnic origin got to do with it or my people — the Yoruba?' He was told to shut up.

They took him back to his cell, which had no bed. Sleeping on the old and dirty brown carpet on a ₦40 meal per day, without access to any reading material or radio, was enough to put Ojudu in a foul mood.

He was not released until the night of July 24, 1998.

On August 18, 1998, Biu, who headed the Task Force on Terrorism held a press conference at Alagbon Close, Ikoyi, Lagos. At that conference, he alleged that Kaltho, who had disappeared in 1996, was the 'unidentified' person who had allegedly planted a bomb at Durbar Hotel on January 18, 1996. He was killed in the process. At the conference, he showed reporters a video cassette of the scene of the blast and two photographs. One was a burnt body who, Biu claimed, was Kaltho. The other was that of Kaltho, as his colleagues knew him. The second piece of evidence, which Biu showed, was a video cassette of an interview by Bauchi Television Authority (BATV) with Buhari in 1994. The cassette was allegedly found at the scene of the blast. Biu said this same interview was published in *TheNEWS* of September 4, 1995, five months before the blast.

In a quick response to Biu, we said at a press conference that Biu was incorrect because when the Durbar Hotel bomb blast occurred on Thursday January 18, 1996 the police immediately moved in to investigate. Newspaper accounts of the blast indicated that the entire vicinity of where it exploded was shattered: that the bomb carrier was burnt beyond recognition. We also said that even Umaru Suleiman, the acting Police Commissioner of Kaduna State at the time, was quoted by *The Guardian*, among several other papers, as saying that the stomach of the victim was 'ripped open, legs shattered and face burnt beyond recognition.'

We concluded that it was very questionable that the face in the photograph given the journalists by Biu had suddenly become recognisable, contrary to the statement made earlier by the police on the matter.

Kaltho, our Kaduna correspondent, contributed to the story, which was the immediate reason for my imprisonment. When I smuggled out a note to my colleagues, warning them that all those who contributed to that story should run for cover, I knew Kaltho would be one of the first to do so because he was security conscious. Kaltho was the only one of all the journalists who wrote to me in jail under a false identity. He had sources within the military, the police and the SSS. He was fond of reading spy books. He did not have talent for elegant prose, but he made up for that by cultivating a zeal for gathering top-secret information. He was very persistent. He was stubborn. His friends in the security helped him to break some exclusive stories but he offended some of them by publishing the stories at a time they did not like.

Babajide Otitoju, who worked with him at our bureau in the north, remembered one particular story: The collapse of the former Inspector-General of Police, Ibrahim Coommasie, at the Murtala Muhammed Square, Kaduna. 'He was reviewing a parade when he slumped. The photographers who wanted to take shots were beaten, their cameras seized and films exposed. Everybody present was ordered not to report it. Kaltho was not at the parade ground. It was our late photographer, Sam Braimoh, who was there. When Braimoh got to the office, he told Kaltho what happened. Being the kind of person he was, Kaltho went ahead and filed the story to Lagos. He wrote that the man was epileptic. Even though Lagos deliberately watered the story down, the police was still furious. I am sure the police did not forgive Kaltho. Each time I discuss with my friends in the north about how Kaltho must have died and I try to link it with the coup story, they would say, 'don't be so sure.' Kaltho offended many people. It would be wrong to look in one direction.'

In those difficult days when *TEMPO* was operating underground, it was Kaltho's connection with the SSS that saved our journalists in Kaduna from being arrested.

Before Olorunyomi left Nigeria on self-exile early 1996, he wrote several cover stories that were critical of the regime of Abacha. It was, therefore, natural that he joined forces with pro-democracy groups abroad. When I caught up with him in his home at Silver Spring in Maryland, USA, in December 1998, I asked why he was not deterred from writing all those critical stories after I had been imprisoned. 'It was because we felt inspired by your sacrifice', he began. 'We owed you a duty to continue that way because we believed that you were not going to compromise with that unrighteous system. There was indeed a vigorous debate about what to do after your imprisonment. Some people thought that we would put you in danger if we continued, but my thinking was that if this guy were here, he would not do otherwise. The talisman for me was the letter you wrote to your wife urging her not to make herself an object of pity. That was what I always quoted to people. You were in jail for what you did not do. You were punished in detention because you were trying to smuggle out a message to warn us. I felt guilty. It became a mission for me, because of that, to fight on'.

Abubakar did not release all the officers who were jailed with us because the majority of those who were serving in his government participated condemning their colleagues to death or sending them to jail*. They never knew that the table would soon turn. Ransome-Kuti, who initiated the joint action to get the officers released, wrote Obasanjo in November 1998, asking him to be part of the effort.

---

* Aziza, for instance, was a Minister in that government.

November 25, 1998

General Olusegun Obasanjo
Obasanjo Farms
Ota,
Ogun State.

Dear General Obasanjo,

CONCERN OVER UNJUST IMPRISONMENT

I wish to express my concern over the fate of several other Nigerians who are unjustly jailed along with your good self and I.

It is now five months since our release was ordered by General Abdulsalami Abubakar, yet nothing has been done about the freedom of these unfortunate fellow citizens. This also applies to General Oladipo Diya and others who have remained in jail over the 1997 coup frame-up.

Consequently, I am suggesting that we should demand for their immediate release by the Federal Government.

Secondly, I am also suggesting we should propose the option of having all of us returned to prison until the government is ready to release everybody involved in both the 1995 and 1997 grand coup frame-ups.

In case the Abubakar regime is not favourably disposed to the demand for their immediate freedom, you may wish to suggest some other option, but I feel it is morally wrong for us to go about as if everything was all right with us.

Thanks in anticipation of your cooperation.

Yours sincerely,
Dr. Beko Ransome-Kuti,
Chairman CD.

December 3, 1998

Dr. Beko Ransome-Kuti
The Chairman, Campaign for Democracy
12 Imaria Street, Anthony Village
P. O. Box 7247, Lagos.

Dear Beko,

RE: CONCERN OVER UNJUST IMPRISONMENT

I acknowledge receipt of your letter of November 25, 1998 regarding our colleagues who were unjustly imprisoned with us and who are still languishing in jail.

Soon after we were released, I raised the issue with the Head of State, General Abubakar. He was not exactly enthusiastic, and he said he would seek the advice of his Attorney-General. It has been several months and he has not got back to me, so it may well be that he is politely declining further action. Of course, you and I know that this is not a matter of legality but correction of injustice.

I also believe that the Head of State is being very cautious because of the fact that all those still incarcerated unjustly were serving officers or other ranks when they were arrested. In the circumstances, we can only continue to pray and bid our time for opportunity for justice to be done. I have no doubt that God is a God of justice and He will open the way for justice to be done. He has done in your case and in my case. He will do it again for those still remaining to be released.

Although the case of Diya and his colleagues may seem to us to be clear instance of miscarriage of justice, there are aspects such as the manner in which they were implicated, that call for different consideration. The fact that the present Head of State and Chief of Defence Staff announced the 'Diya Coup', and as Head of State commuted the death sentence to 25 years imprisonment less than five months ago, may not make it easy for him to be able to grant them reprieve. Again, I have already taken this issue up with him. And I would like to suggest that we be patient.

But if our individual efforts have failed to yield the desired result, I am prepared to support a suitable joint action. I am afraid I am of the opinion that your proposal as it stands is unlikely to be effective in achieving our objective. My suggestion is that we should write a cogent letter of appeal to the Head of State, in which the two cases are distinguished and argued for separately. If he has any inhibition, such a letter may strengthen his hand for positive reaction. I am willing to append my signature to such a serious letter whose purpose is more than the publicity effect.

We should also offer to be ready to meet the Head of State on the issue, if he would be kind enough to offer us an invitation. Such a letter should not be made public before we have got a response from him or before we have intimated him with our intention to publicise it and the reasons for doing so.

If you agree to my suggestion, please canvass the idea among those of us who have been released, then let me have the first draft of the letter of appeal for my comments and approval. The letter should have the addresses of all the signatories so that the reply could be sent to either of us or simultaneously to all of us.

I look forward to hearing from you.
Olusegun Obasanjo

After this exchange, the two of them met. At this meeting, Obasanjo told Ransome-Kuti that he had been advised to write his own appeal because he had been assured that such appeal would bring quick result. The following is Obasanjo's appeal:

January 6, 1999

His Excellency General Abdulsalami Abubakar
Head of State of the Federal Republic of Nigeria
Abuja

APPEAL FOR PRISONERS HELD FOR ALLEGED INVOLVEMENT IN **1995** AND **1997** COUP PLOTS

I am constrained at the beginning of this New Year, which is billed to be a year of blessing for all Nigerians, to further plead in writing as a continuation of earlier verbal pleadings for the prisoners still held for alleged involvement in plotting the overthrow of the military government in 1995 and 1997.

I am particularly conscious not just of the devastating effects of losing one's personal freedom but more so to lose that inalienable right of every individual human being in palpably unjust circumstances. In the spirit of suffering camaraderie, I cannot but continue to appeal for the release of these Nigerians who are clearly fellow victims of the same injustice done to me and which you have ameliorated somewhat.

If, as I believe, your decision to release me together with some other prisoners was based on your recognition of the injustice done to us, then your effort to right the wrong is hardly complete if any of those unjustly incarcerated with

us are still being held six months after we have regained our freedom. As long as these persons remain in detention, our own freedom feels hollow and unfulfilled. I am sure you meant fulfillment.

Whatever may be the security consideration in the cases of these prisoners still being held, I believe that talking to them and keeping surveillance on them ought to be sufficient measure. I am hereby making a special appeal, on my own behalf and on behalf of other comrades already released, for an urgent review of the circumstances of these people still incarcerated with a view to releasing them in the immediate future. It will also be another step in the right direction for improving the image of Nigeria.

Thank you for giving consideration to this appeal.

Olusegun Obasanjo

On February 23, 1999, Ransome-Kuti called a press conference at which he said that Obasanjo's suggestion that those who were in jail should be kept under surveillance upon their release was morally reprehensible. He said it was unfair to assume that the victims were being held in prison for the security of Abubakar. He called on the government to state under which law the victims were still being held. He concluded by demanding immediate freedom for all the remaining victims of the 1995 and 1997 coup plots 'or in the alternative all the freed victims, including Obasanjo, should be sent back to jail.'

The officers were eventually released on March 4, 1999.

A heavy burden is lifted. My wound is healed. I am happy to be alive to share my stories with you.

Appendices

The 1995 Coup Victims*

1.	Ex-Major Akinloye Akinyemi	Kaduna Prison
2.	Col. Lawan Gwadabe	Maximum Security Prison, Kirikiri, Lagos
3.	Col. O. Oloruntoba	Calabar Prison
4.	Col. R.S.B. Bello-Fadile	Maximum Security Prison, Potiskum
5.	Lt-Col. K. H. Bulus	Enugu Prison
6.	Lt-Col. S. E. Oyewole	Yola Prison
7.	Col. E. I. Ndubueze	Abeokuta Prison
8.	Col. G.A. Ajayi	Minna Prison
9.	Col. R. N. Emokpae	Maximum Security Prison, Birni-Kebbi
10.	Lt-Col. M.A. Igwe	Jalingo Prison
11.	Maj. D. O. Obalisa	Bauchi Prison
12.	Lt. A. Olowookere	Wukari Prison
13.	Lt-Col. M.A. Ajayi (rtd.)	Maiduguri Prison

---

* Some of the victims were later moved to other prisons.

14.	Gen. S.M. Yar'Adua (rtd.)	Port Harcourt Prison
15.	Gen. O. Obasanjo	Jos Prison
16.	Capt. M. A. Ibrahim	Akure Prison
17.	2Lt. R. Emouvhe	Kano Prison
18.	Sgt. Patrick Usikpeko	Uyo Prison
19.	Mallam Shehu Sani	Aba Prison
20.	Mr. Ben Charles-Obi	Agodi Prison, Ibadan.
21.	Alhaji Sanusi Mato	Owerri Prison
22.	Mr. Felix Ndamaigida	Ilesha Prison
23.	Mr. Julius Badejo	Gusau Prison
24.	Mrs. Chris Anyanwu	Gombe Prison
25.	Mr. Mathew Popoola	Mubi Prison
26.	Mr. George Mbah	Biu Prison
27.	Mr. Kunle Ajibade	Makurdi Prison
28.	Cdr. L.M.O. Fabiyi	Sokoto Prison
29.	Mr. Moses Ayegba	Benin Prison
30.	Miss Rebecca Onyabi Ikpe	Zaria Prison
31.	Dr. Beko Ransome-Kuti	Katsina Prison
32.	Lt-Col. R.D. Obiki	Gboko Prison
33.	Lt-Col. O.E. Nyong	Gashua Prison

34.	Lt-Col. C.P. Izourgu	Ilorin Prison
35.	Cpl. Godspower Ogbonnaya	Argungu Prison
36.	Capt. A. A. Ogunsuyi	Umuahia Prison
37.	Lt-Col. V. O. Bamgbose	Awka Prison
38.	Maj. I.D. Edeh	Kontagora Prison
39.	Lt-Col. S.B. Mapaiyeda	Onitsha Prison
40.	Miss Queenette Lewis-Allagoa	Maximum Security Prison, Kirikiri, Lagos
41.	L.Cpl Joseph Onwe	Keffi Prison

FALANA AND FALANA'S CHAMBERS
Barristers, Solicitors & Legal Consultants

PRACTITIONERS
alana, LL.B (Ife) B.L
ınye LL B (Ben) B.L.
Falana B.Sc (Ben) LL.B (Lag) B.L, LL.M
Hart Olekanma LL.B. (Ife) B.L
ı Joseph LL.B (Lag) B.L
Maduabuchi LLB (Ife) B.L
ıgbinoba LL.B (Ekp) B.L
Obafemi LL.B (Ife) B.L

Suite A (1st Floor)
Obafemi Awolowo House,
29/31 Obafemi Awolowo Way.
Ikeja, Lagos.
Tel/Fax : 234-1-4936907
: 234-1-7752202

: REF: FF/2000/

⁄ 5, 2000

ef Bola Ige (S.A.N)
ıourable Attorney - General
/linister of Justice
eral Ministry of Justice
eral Secretariat
ıja.

ır Sir,

PARDON FOR KUNLE AJIBADE, CHRIS ANYANWU, GEORGE MBAH, BEN CHARLES - OBI AND SHEHU SANNI

are Solicitors to **KUNLE AJIBADE, CHRIS ANYANWU, GEORGE MBAH, BEN ARLES OBI** and **SHEHU SANNI** (hereinafter referred to as "our clients") on ɔse instructions we write this letter.

clients' have briefed us as follows:-

That at different times in 1995 our clients were arrested and detained at the Directorate of Military Intelligence Apapa, Lagos for their alleged complicity in the phantom coup against the defunct Sani Abacha junta.

That in the course of investigation our clients vehemently denied any involvement in the phantom coup.

That to the utter dismay of our clients they were arraigned before the Patrick Aziza Special Military Tribunal set up by the then Provisional Ruling Council to try all suspects roped into the phantom coup.

That without any scintilla of evidence linking our clients with the phantom coup the said Special Military Tribunal convicted them of the offences of conspiracy and treasonable felony and sentenced them to life imprisonment which was reduced to 15 years jail term by the Abacha junta.

SOCIAL JUSTICE FOR ALL

5. That for over three years our clients were held in dehumanizing conditions at military camps and prisons in various parts of the country.

6. That our clients were among the scores of political prisoners released in July 1998 on the orders of the then Military Head of State, General Abdulsalami Abubakar.

7. That in exercise of his powers under Section 175 of the Constitution of the Federal Republic of Nigeria, 1999 President Olusegun Obasanjo recently granted full pardon to our clients.

8. That even though our clients wholeheartedly appreciate the kind gesture of President Obasanjo in granting them pardon they feel highly embarrased that they have been pardoned for offences they never committed.

In the light of the foregoing we have the firm instructions of our clients to demand for the setting up of a judicial panel to review their illegal arrest, detention, trial and conviction with a view to setting aside same and recommending appropriate punishment for all the public officers who roped them into the phantom coup and had them jailed in a desperate bid to silence a critical segment of the Nigerian society.

In particular our clients deserve to be adequately compensated having regard to the fact that military officers who were convicted in similar circumstances have had their ranks and benefits restored to them following the pardon recently granted them by the President.

It is hoped that our clients' demands herein will be favourably considered by the Federal Government without any delay. Otherwise our clients reserve the right to seek redress in the law court to relieve themselves of the psychological trauma and physical brutalities meted to them for over three years without any justification whatsoever.

Yours Sincerely,

FEMI FALANA

ATTORNEY-GENERAL OF THE FEDERATION AND MINISTER OF JUSTICE

P.M.B. 192
Telegrams: Solicitor
Telephone: 09-5235194
Telefax: 09-5235208

Federal Ministry of Justice
10th Floor, Federal Secretariat
Shehu Shagari Way
Maitama, Abuja, FCT
Nigeria

HAGF/MISC/2000/Vol.I/

18th July, 2000

Mr. Femi Falana,
Falana & Falana's Chambers,
Suite A (1st Floor)
Obafemi Awolowo House,
29/31 Obafemi Awolowo Way,
Ikeja – Lagos

Dear Mr. Falana,

Re: PARDON FOR KUNLE AJIBADE, CHRIS ANYANWU, GEORGE MBAH, CHARLES BEN OBI AND SHEHU SANNI

Your letter Ref. FF/2000 of July 5 refers.

2.   You will recall that one of the major initiatives of this administration was to set up a judicial enquiry under the chairmanship of Hon. Justice C. Oputa (rtd) into alleged cases of Human Rights violations by previous regimes, from 1976 till today. Other than this panel, the National Human Rights Commission is empowered by Act No. 22 of 1995 to investigate cases of Human Rights violation and recommend appropriate redress.

3.   In the light of these, it would amount to unnecessary duplicity if a judicial panel is set up to look into your clients' grievances, which fall squarely within the mandate of these bodies.

4.   My counsel to you therefore is that you should formally present these grievances to either or both bodies.

Yours sincerely,

CHIEF BOLA IGE, SAN
Attorney-General of the Federation and
Minister of Justice

Index